AFTERSHOCKS

AN OLD BARN BOOK
First published in the UK, Australia and New Zealand in 2022 by
Old Barn Books Ltd
West Sussex
RH20 1JW

9781910646823
eBook ISBN: 9781910646793

1 3 5 7 9 10 8 6 4 2

Old Barn Books Ltd is an independent UK-based publisher of picture books and fiction
www.oldbarnbooks.com
Follow us on Facebook, Twitter or Instagram: @oldbarnbooks

We are proud to be distributed in the UK by Bounce Sales & Marketing Ltd
www.bouncemarketing.co.uk
and in Australia and New Zealand by Walker Books Australia
www.walkerbooks.com.au

An audio version of this book is available
from Bolinda Publishing
www.bolinda.com

Design and typesetting by Tracey Cunnell
Editor: Emma Roberts
Cover design and illustration by David and Lydia Ellwand
With thanks to Jake and Robbie

FSC® helps take care of forests for future generations
Printed and bound by CPI Group (UK) Ltd, Croydon, CR0 4YY

AFTERSHOCKS

Anne Fine

Dad dropped me off at Mum's, but even before I'd scrambled out of the car, she was frantically waving at both of us from the kitchen window.

'Don't drive away,' I warned. 'I'm pretty sure she wants to tell you something.'

I saw it on his face: *Oh, Lord! What have I done wrong now?*

Mum hurried to the kerbside. 'You can't leave Louie here. No, not tonight. Or tomorrow.'

'But it's Thursday.'

'I know it's Thursday, Philip. But first thing in the morning I'll be off on my walking weekend and won't be back till Monday night.'

'You should have told me.'

She put on her *gotcha!* look. 'I did tell you, Philip.

First I *asked* you, and you agreed to switch the days around. That was two months ago. I reminded you two weeks ago, and then again on Monday.' She gave him a triumphant smile. 'Would you like to see the screenshots?'

He'd lost the battle so he tried another tack. 'Well, can't you take him with you?'

'I'm not going walking with Mum's friends!' I said. 'They spend their whole time teasing me.' (I would have added, '*And* they walk too fast,' but that would have sounded pathetic.)

'Why don't I drive you round to Will's?'

'No chance,' I said. 'His gran's there this weekend.'

'Just take him back,' said Mum, as if I were some mongrel dog that Dad had unaccountably picked up from a rescue centre and tried to dump at her place.

'Anna, I can't,' Dad said. 'I'm off on an inspection.'

'Well, take him with you.'

'I can't,' he said again. 'It's way out east. Some godforsaken hole in the old Endlands. It's going to take a full four days. Possibly even longer.'

'Then make sure he packs his toothbrush,' Mum said cheerily.

And she was gone.

ONE

On the way to Nowhere-on-Stilts

Dad said he'd never been to the Causeway Pumping Station before. He remembered that he'd been scheduled to do the function and safety checks there a few years earlier, but in the end someone else was given that assignment and he'd been packed off somewhere else.

He didn't know much about the place. Everyone knew that the Endlands were horribly isolated, out there on the very furthest edge of the country. And dull. One rubbish road to get there. Not much when you arrived. No pizza places or cinemas. Nothing to do in the evenings.

'Good job it's one of the simplest pumping stations in the country,' Swati kept telling the three who made up the inspection team. 'The equipment's so basic that you can be in and out of the plant well before you go stark, staring crazy.'

So we would be four on the trip. My dad, Valentina and Miles – and now me. Everyone turned a blind eye to the backpack I'd dumped in the corner of the equipment shed, and pretended they didn't know that I'd be coming along. Swati's no idiot, and she's been Chief Coordinator of Inspection Teams for ages now. But Dad still somehow managed to give her the impression that I was just hitching a lift a mile or so along the road, as far as the house of a friend.

I sat on a humming generator thing and watched them as they got their act together. Dad went through the inventory to make sure they'd remembered all their bits of equipment. Miles was sorting out the packages of pre-packed food in case the very few tiny shops that were supposed to be along the start of the route all happened to be closed. Hardly anyone goes to the Endlands, and what we learn about them in school would put you off going anyway. Swati had warned us that anywhere more than a hundred miles east of Highway Five, the population live entirely by their own means and keep to their own rules. 'They're a bit weird,' she said.

2

Miles clearly felt obliged to make the obvious joke. 'Well, we should fit in well. We're all a bit weird, too.'

'Not the way those people are,' Swati had muttered. So Miles was packing up a heap of basic foodstuffs, and a few treats to keep us going. Swati made sure the works garage gave us the most dependable of the vehicles.

'Any trouble,' she warned us, 'and you'll be stuck out there for ever. You're pretty well on the way to Nowhere-on-Stilts.'

She waved our van out of the storage hangar, towards the massive gates. And off we went.

TWO

Toby's gone now

The drive took far, far longer than expected. Once we were off the highway and into the protected wilderness, the road was poor – enough bank slides and potholes to slow us down a lot. It dwindled to a one-lane track much sooner than suggested by the map. That wasn't too much of a hindrance – there didn't seem to be much traffic coming the other way. I doubt if, in the many hours that we were in the van, we met more than a dozen vehicles, and only once did we have to back up to let a lorry past.

After we left the last tiny roadside garage, the flickering of glare and shade that had been so mesmeric gave way to thicker, darker forest. The air was steamy, and every tree trunk appeared to be coated in strangely shaped lichens and fungi.

'Nothing but mould and mildew,' Miles complained.

'At least you're safe in the van,' said Valentina. 'When I drove through before, I made the big mistake of going for a walk. I came back reckoning that every single living creature for miles around had taken the chance to startle me or bite me or sting me, and every plant I walked past was out to scratch or strangle me.'

Miles stared out into the still-deepening shadows. 'It's all so *dense*. Mile after mile of dark green forest. No villages. No farms. No tiny homesteads. Not even any clearings. Why aren't there any *people*?'

'Pretty well all of the Endlanders fetched up in the small villages strung out along the Causeway Bay,' said Valentina.

'Where we're going?'

'A tiny bit further than that. They're on the far side of the coastal ridge.'

'But what on earth do they *live* on?' Miles wailed. (He sounded so anxious that suddenly I had an inkling why Dad and Valentina had left him in charge of packing all our food.)

'Fish, mostly,' Valentina told him. 'Fish that they catch themselves. In fact, you only have to spend a few hours there to reckon that everyone along the bay seems to belong more to the sea than the land.'

'Like seals,' Miles said. 'Or mermaids.'

'They do have boats,' said Valentina tartly, as if she thought Miles was so dense he wouldn't have realised. 'They use them for everything. Up till a few years ago there wasn't even a road along the coastal side of the ridge. Everything and everyone had to go along the beach. I saw a painting in the art gallery at Sachard that showed all these carts and donkeys and clusters of people passing one another on the sands.'

I'm sure she would have told us more, but it was obvious that, at the mere mention of an art gallery, Miles had lost interest. He started hunting noisily around his feet for one of the packets of biscuits he'd stowed there before we set off. I took the shortbread whirls he offered me and went back to staring out at the strange mosses dangling from the trees in long and wispy strands, as if the grey fluff of a thousand vacuum cleaner bags had been emptied out over their branches.

The three of them took turns to drive. Both Dad and Valentina were steady enough, but all of us got tense when Miles took over. His steering was erratic. It was as if his mind, like mine, had drifted somewhere else. But I have an excuse. When I'm in any sort of vehicle

7

I can't help thinking about my brother Toby, two years older than me, and killed by a tearaway driver over a year ago. So Toby's gone now. But we had all those years of sitting next to one another in cars, bickering and sleeping, complaining about how bored we were, or playing stupid games. I'm getting better at feeling that I'm doing all right by myself in other places now. But in the back seat of a car, I always feel as if one half of me is torn away. I feel half-empty.

Why don't I simply say it? I feel *crap*.

I'm glad that Dad took over the driving again as dusk was settling in. Miles got out to change places and, as he did so, a chocolate wrapper that had been stuck to his trainer in the footwell of the van was ripped away by the breeze and floated along the track.

Valentina saw. 'Hey!' she said sharply as he set off around the van to get in the other side. 'Better go get it.'

So, Miles chased after it and picked it up. He got back in, making a face that as good as said, *fusspot!* My dad stuck up for Valentina as he slid the van back into gear by carolling Mum's walking group's jingle, 'Leave only footprints, take only memories.'

'Who'd want to remember this creepy place?' said Miles. And I could see his point. It was the most unnerving forest I'd ever driven through. All of the trees that we were passing now seemed to be crouched on massive twisted roots that stood high off the ground, as if at any moment, when it was fully dark, they might rise up and stride about the way they do in horror films. Each time we caught a glimpse of the rising moon, it looked far larger than it should have done, and swarms of bloated bats whirled overhead.

'Spooky,' I knew my brother would be saying. He would be loving every minute. 'Seriously weird.'

In front of us, the spiky blue silhouette of the coastal range drew closer. 'Good thing they built the pumping station this side,' Dad said. 'I wouldn't fancy driving over the top of that ridge in the pitch dark.'

'What's there to see, in any case?' Miles muttered grumpily.

Valentina took what he'd said more as a question than a complaint about the posting Swati had chosen for them. 'Apart from the string of tiny coastal villages? Not much,' she admitted. 'Fishermen and upturned boats. Nets spread to dry. Most of the locals wearing the sort of drab, baggy clothes you'd put on to clear out your attic. Old people hobbling about with woven baskets.' There was a moment's pause. 'And everyone staring, of course.'

'Staring?'

'Yes. People in the Endlands are always staring. They almost seem to make a point of acting as if strangers are something quite out of the ordinary.'

'When aeroplanes were new,' I said, remembering something my great-grandmother once told me, 'everyone stopped and pointed when they flew overhead.'

'Yes, rather like that, I suppose,' said Valentina. 'But more unnerving, somehow, because of the *way* they're looking.'

'The way they're looking?'

I honestly don't think Valentina noticed the little shudder she gave as she began to explain. 'I think it might be partly the colour of their eyes. They're blue, but it's a rather washed-out, watery blue. They can look so *expressionless* – so cold and blank. You see them watching and you get the shivers. But I can see why they might be so guarded. We were the enemy for so long, and treated them so badly.' She shrugged. 'They are an odd lot altogether, to be frank.'

I do biology in school. 'How come they have blue eyes?' I asked. 'Blue eyes are totally rare now.'

I got the feeling that my question made Valentina uncomfortable. But she explained. 'Endlanders never mixed. So it's not just the eyes. They're also almost all astonishingly tall and thin, with bone-white faces. Almost bloodless-looking. And they have spindly legs, and wrists and arms like glass rods. They are so colourless you'd think they never saw the sun at all, let alone spend most of their lives fishing along the bay.'

'They sound like *ghouls*,' said Miles. 'Oh, I am really looking forward to this trip!' It was the third thing in a row he'd said to make it clear he wasn't happy. I couldn't work Miles out at all. Dad always said he was a first-class engineer 'for somebody his age' (though Miles was well into his twenties). But then Dad also claimed he sometimes acted as if he was no older than eight and had never learned how to grow up. Dad even told me Swati had to think the teams out very carefully because some people hated to work with him. 'The way he deals with people gets on their nerves.'

So, Miles was often paired with Valentina and my dad because they were both middle-aged and sensible. Valentina comes from one of those old Russian provinces. Mum says that, with those high Slavic cheekbones and raven black hair, she's absolutely beautiful, but Dad treats her simply as a mate – just engineers together, doing a job they love.

We drove on for a good few miles. Then, rounding a bend, without a moment's warning, nearly came off the track.

'What the—?'

Dad hit the brakes so hard that we were all thrown forward. Without the seat belts, I reckon Valentina and Dad would have gone straight through the windscreen. 'What on *earth*?'

'Scary!'

It was, too. Now that we'd all had time to get a grip and look up, I could see what had freaked Dad. Looming above us was a massive face carved in the mountain rock. And what a face! Thin and cadaverous, but the height of a house. Even in the poor light, the pale grey stone from which the image had been cut gave it a grim, unhealthy look. The face's huge wide eyes peered down at us as if we were mere beetles on the road. Its mouth was open, twisted in a way that made me feel we should be hearing some giant roar of agony echoing round us.

Dad shoved the vehicle into reverse. We skidded back. 'Steady on, Philip,' Valentina warned. 'It's only a face on the rock. It's not going to bend down and eat you.'

Beside me, Miles was chuckling. 'A rock face on a rock face.'

Dad made an effort to calm down, and we drove on.

'Why's it there, anyway?' Miles asked after a while. He flipped his hair back, but it was such a mop it fell forward straightaway. 'Was it some sort of warning, like those huge statues that stare out from Easter Island?'

'I think those are simply images of ancient kings,' Dad said.

'Maybe they are,' Miles shrugged. 'I don't know anything about primitive art. But I bet if that scary face had been carved anywhere less off the beaten track, people would know about it well before it startled them halfway to death as they drove round that corner. They would have seen a dozen billboards on the way, telling them about it.'

'Yes, actually – you could have *warned* me,' Dad grumbled to Valentina. 'You must have seen it when you were here before.'

'I expect I was so freaked by all the ruts and potholes in the track, I never raised my eyes to notice it.'

But it had given all of us a shock, and I was glad when we drove round a few more bends and saw the pumping station up ahead, tucked in a fold of the ridge.

THREE

Don't tempt the gods

The station seemed to be pretty much as those three expected, but I was baffled. 'Why was it built in the first place? What's round here to pump?'

'Water,' Dad told me.

'I can't see any.'

'We crossed the river further back,' Valentina reminded me. 'Here, it runs underground, under the ridge to the sea.'

'Doesn't that make moving the water harder?'

'Not really.' And she went on to explain. I think she must have forgotten that I'm not one of her apprentices, I'm just Dad's son, because I didn't understand a word. In fact, though I kept saying, 'Ah!', and nodding my head politely, I soon stopped listening. In any case, by then we'd drawn up outside the perimeter fence. After a minute or two, a tall, skinny man with sunken cheeks stumbled out of the gatehouse, lit by the moonlight. He didn't even glance our way, though he was clearly coming towards the gate.

'Now, there's a man who lives on misery sandwiches,' Miles muttered as we watched him heave aside the rusty chain and fiddle with the lock. 'Gloomy or what?'

Valentina sighed. '*Everyone* round here is gloomy. And with some reason, when you come to think of it.'

By now the sour-looking caretaker had turned his back on us. My only guess was that he must have brought the wrong key. While he was walking back towards the gatehouse, in no great hurry, I took the chance to ask, 'What happened to them, then?'

'Same as all over,' Valentina said. 'They must have taught you about the Annexation of the Provinces? Here, it got pretty nasty because this place had been a kingdom of its own, with its own religion and customs and laws. But after they were taken over—'

'Conquered,' Dad broke in to correct her. 'Smashed by superior forces, then left to rot.'

I did remember being taught about how the Federation was brought together, bit by bit. Ms Nyland had gone on about how everyone in the Cities and the

16

Central Belt were sure they were doing the far-flung people who lived in the High Islands and the Endlands a favour by conquering them. *Bringing them civilization,* I remember her saying. But after that, she'd added, almost as an afterthought, *But we do tend to look at these things rather differently now.* So I already must have at least half-known the story Valentina and Dad were telling me. It's just I hadn't clocked that one of those smaller outer provinces we'd studied in our Federation History class was actually this place.

'And after that,' Valentina was admitting, 'they had a hard time of it.'

Now I was a lot more interested than I had been in school. 'What sort of hard time?'

'Oh, you know.' She made a face. 'The usual. The women shipped off to the Cities as poorly paid servants and worse. Their men shoved in the front line to catch the fire first in all the wars and battles. And the very few who were left, the coastal fishermen, paid almost nothing for their catches.'

I thought about it. Now it was obvious why the thin, sullen caretaker had not so much as raised a hand to greet us before he'd started fumbling with the lock. For him, and all the families around, we probably were still the old, old enemy; nothing but bad news and trouble.

'How can he take so *long?*' demanded Miles. 'He *works* here. He must open these gates twice a day.'

I pointed to a rusty bike against the fence. 'Maybe he just climbs over. Or squeezes through that hole.'

Dad sighed. 'Item the first. Get the security fence mended.'

The caretaker came back at last. Again, he fiddled with a key, and this time the padlock fell open. He slowly dragged the metal gates back far enough for Dad to drive inside. We saw the building clearly in the moonlight. It was a solid, blocky shape built hard up against the ridge. The compound round it looked as drab and empty as a prison yard.

Dad scrambled stiffly out of the driving seat. 'I'm going to ask him to switch on the lights and show us round.'

Miles groaned. 'What, now? Tonight?'

'Yes,' Dad said. 'Tonight. In case there are quirks in the system that he might otherwise forget to mention. And then I'm going to give him the full three days off.'

'Smart!' Miles admitted. 'Having that man watch

18

every move we make would scarcely be a pleasure.'

I turned to look, and it was true that the caretaker was staring at us in the most unnerving way. His huge blank eyes looked almost bleached in the pale light.

'He does appear quite menacing,' my dad agreed. 'But maybe he's not sure quite why we're here.'

Dad went across to tell the caretaker the deal. The man showed not the slightest sign of gratitude or pleasure at the idea of three days off. But he did speed up his act. After he'd shown Dad the lights, and opened up the inner sections of the building, it was no time at all before he'd gathered what he wanted from the gatehouse. He clearly didn't want to call attention to the hole in the fence he'd either made for his own convenience or never bothered to repair, so he went out through the gates. Handing the bunch of keys to Valentina, he made straight for the rusty bike I'd noticed earlier. He was so tall and thin that when he rode off into the night, he looked more like a scarecrow than a man.

'Miserable sourpuss,' said Miles.

I watched as the caretaker and his bike were swallowed by the dark between the trees. 'Where is he going?' I asked Valentina.

'I expect he's off over the ridge to spend the time with his family.'

I looked up at the jagged shadow looming over us. 'Over *that*? On a *bike*? In the pitch *dark*?' (I mean, Will and I fancy ourselves as pretty good off-roaders, but this was ridiculous.)

She laughed. 'He'll dump the bike a little further along, where there's a sort of easy climb – almost a footpath – over to the bay.'

She pushed the gates together while Dad and Miles went back towards the pumping station door.

'Why are you bothering to lock them again?' I asked her. 'No one's around.'

'Firm's rules,' she said. 'Some of the work plants in the Endlands have a history of sabotage.'

We turned to follow Dad and Miles. Halfway across the compound, I felt vibrations under my feet and stopped to point. 'What's that?'

'That hum? That's from the pumps. The water we're diverting runs under where you're standing.'

It seemed a little late to ask the question, but I did. 'Why divert water if there's almost nothing round here?'

Valentina tossed back her hair and scooped it

more tightly into the purple band she used to keep it off her face. 'Because the firm is paid to get a lot of it up to Topane.' She saw my blank face. 'That's a small community a few miles further along the ridge.'

We don't just study our Federation's history at school. We do earth sciences as well. 'Why would a small community get started in a place which has no water of its own?'

'Rare metals. Topane's an important mine.' By now, we'd caught up with the other two, and she brought Dad into the conversation. 'Phil, does this son of yours ever run out of questions?'

Dad reached out to ruffle my hair as if I were a five year old. 'Oh, Louie's like that. Happy to sit for hours saying nothing, then turns into the Chief Inquisitor.'

The three of them took off to wander through the plant. I tagged along. I didn't follow much of what they said, but I still got the feeling that they thought the system was dead simple, and it was mostly going to be a matter of checking for hairline cracks in pipes and doing basic servicing. Just as we worked our way back round to where we'd started, Miles said, 'I'm not sure why they had to send the three of us. I reckon any competent apprentice could make a fair stab at this job.'

'That is the sort of remark,' said Dad, 'that tends to lead to trouble.'

Startled, Miles asked, 'What do you mean by that?'

But it was Valentina who answered him. 'Don't tempt the gods,' she warned Miles. 'Philip is telling you never to tempt the gods.'

FOUR

Spi Ruaradh

'We'll start tomorrow,' Dad told them. 'Bring in the stuff you need overnight. Louie and I can put our sleeping mats inside the engine room. Valentina, do you fancy using the caretaker's bed? It probably has a proper mattress.'

She gave a delicate shudder. 'No, thanks. I'll use a sleeping mat as well.'

'I'd take his bed,' said Miles, 'except I don't want to sleep in that gatehouse by myself. Too near those creepy trees.' He wandered off to fetch the cold box from the van and found somewhere to plug it in. Cheerfully it whirred back to life.

'What have you got in there?' I asked. (We had been snacking all the way, but I was still hungry.)

'Pies. Sandwiches. Wraps. Juice. Milk. Fruit.' His

eyes lit up. 'And, with a bit of luck, if the baby generator in the van was doing its stuff on the way, a couple of tubs of ice cream.'

I was astonished. Taking two huge wraps – one for me and one for Dad – out of Miles's store, I asked him, '*Ice cream?*'

He grinned. 'Why not? We're near the seaside, after all. We might not get to see it, but it can't be more than half a mile away, over the ridge.'

Just then, Dad called to us from the passage outside. 'Hey! Come and look at these.'

We found him standing by a line of photographs – framed black and white things, presumably from when the plant was built. I didn't realise for a while that they were in sequence, showing construction from the very start, because we went along the passageway looking at them in reverse order. The one we gathered round first was proudly labelled *Causeway Pumping Station*, and showed about thirty lanky, spectre-thin labourers standing in uneven lines in front of the finished building. These workers were flanked on either side by a few shorter, more solid-looking men wearing trousers with turn-ups and the sort of old-fashioned jackets that had leather elbow patches.

'Those will have been the professionals,' Dad said. 'The architect. The principal engineer. The chief of works. Those sorts of bods.'

'They look pretty pleased with themselves,' I said.

'And fair enough. Back then, just getting the materials and equipment into this benighted area must have been quite an extraordinary achievement, let alone building the place.'

'The rest of them don't look too happy,' Miles observed. And he was right. Not one of the workmen's thin, unsmiling faces showed even a hint of the sort of satisfaction you'd expect to see when people who have worked together for months finally complete a task. These labourers looked not just embarrassed – as if this business of a formal photograph was both unusual and most unwelcome – but sullen too.

Shifty, almost.

'A most uneasy bunch,' agreed Valentina, 'attempting to hide the evidence.'

I hadn't noticed up till then, but she was right. When you looked closely, you could see that some of the workers were trying to conceal the tools of their trade in the folds of their overalls, or behind their backs. Presumably someone in charge had asked them to display a few token claw-hammers and pipe wrenches and stuff, but they were obviously unhappy about this proof of their involvement in the project.

We wandered back in time along the series of photos, watching the roof of the pumping station disappear and its massive side walls gradually getting lower. Untidy scatterings of cut pipe gradually grew in length, to finally be seen stacked in their original piles. Elsewhere in the compound, untidy, leftover heaps of sand and cement increased in size along the line of photographs, till each became a massive, freshly delivered mountain, before both suddenly vanished with no trace.

By then, of course, we knew that we were standing in front of what had been the very first photo. The chosen site. A section of untouched ground, hard up against the ridge fold. There was faint spidery writing underneath, and I could just make out the words *Spi Ruaradh.*

I hadn't got the slightest idea how to pronounce it, so I pointed. 'What does that mean?'

Dad turned to Valentina. 'Over to you. You're the local expert.'

She made a face. 'I haven't the least idea.'

'And why,' I asked her, 'did they decide to build the station right up against the ridge, with all the extra bother of blocking off that cave or tunnel, or whatever.'

'What cave? What tunnel?'

Again I pointed, and they peered more closely at the dark and twisted shadow on the ridge.

'Creepy,' said Miles. 'It's the exact same shape as that weird face we saw.'

I hadn't realised till he spoke. But, yes. The shadow was the same long and cadaverous shape, down to an even darker patch that matched the weirdly gaping mouth we'd seen on the rock face.

But it was something else that interested Dad. 'Louie's quite right. It does seem odd to choose to build the station hard up against a rock irregularity like that.'

'No way of finding out the reason now,' said Miles.

I said, 'That caretaker might know.'

Dad brushed off the idea. 'Too long ago. He wouldn't have been around.'

But Valentina backed me up. 'He'll have been *told*. That's what they do to pass the time in dead-end places like these. They endlessly chew over the small potatoes

27

of their ancestors' past lives. While he was growing up, his grandparents probably bored him over and over with every detail of the building of this plant.'

'We must remember to ask him when he gets back.'

He never did come back. We never saw the caretaker again.

FIVE

There might be aftershocks

The earthquake happened the following morning, just after dawn. All night, the steady throbbing of the motors in the engine room had threaded through my dreams, and each time the ventilators sprang to life, pulling in more damp air, I found myself stirring in my sleep. This new noise started as a rumble in my dream, no more than the sound of a motorbike powering along in the distance, and didn't wake me till it became the sort of grating roar that no one could keep working into a dream.

Next moment, Dad was shaking me. 'Wake up! Wake up!'

'I *am* awake!'

'Then use your sense! Get up! Get out!'

The others were already at the doorway. He spun

round and yelled at them. 'Go. Get outside! We're coming!' He turned back. 'For God's sake, Louie! Move!'

I reached for my backpack. 'Leave it!' he yelled, dragging me to my feet and tugging me after him along the passage towards the main door. It was already swinging closed behind the other two. I started to say, 'I thought you were supposed to stay *inside* in earthquakes,' but the noise around us had become so ear-splitting, I wasn't sure if Dad knew I'd so much as opened my mouth.

Even before we reached the door, it had buckled and jammed. Together, we tried to push it open. It scraped a tiny bit further over the floor, then juddered to a halt. I stood there like a dope, not knowing what to do, but Dad didn't hang about. He stepped back several paces, then charged the door, turning at the last moment to hurl his shoulder at it like a battering ram, driving it open a hand's width more.

It was enough. 'Get *through*,' he shouted. '*Push* yourself, Louie! Get *through*.'

Somehow, I managed it, and so did he.

We crossed the compound. That wasn't easy, either. The ground was not just trembling, it was almost *bucking* under our feet, and there was the most deafening roar all round that made me stupidly keep turning to see what it was that seemed to be storming up behind.

At last, we reached the others, who stood unsteadily beside the gates.

'Move aside!' Dad yelled. 'You don't want to be next to that fence when it buckles and snaps.'

We all moved back. I put my mouth against his ear and shouted, 'I thought you were supposed to stay *inside* in earthquakes.'

Either he didn't hear, or he ignored me. And when I turned to look, I saw an avalanche of rocks tumbling like spilled rice down the face of the ridge on to the pumping station's roof. The ground jolted badly again. The solid walls in front of us rippled like water, and then collapsed from top to bottom in strangely folding loops of mortar and brick. Above the grinding noise still splitting the air, I heard one fierce *bang*, like a gun shot, then another and another. Behind us, as Dad had warned, the metal posts were bursting from the ground, the lengths of fencing between them ripping apart as easily as if they were fusty old bedsheets rather than squares of steel.

'Watch out!'

With a hideous crack, the ground in front of us snaked open. Valentina and Dad pulled me back and Miles jumped to safety on the other side.

The roar grew even louder. How long since it started? I had completely lost track. It felt like hours, and yet no time at all. But, in the end, the worst of it did seem to be over. I gradually uncurled. Dad took his trembling arm from round my shoulders. Not one of us could talk for coughing. I blinked grit out of my eyes and tried to look at the others. Their arms and legs and faces, along with the shorts and T-shirts they'd been sleeping in, were all, like mine, coated in fine grey dust.

I couldn't help it, I just thought of Toby. 'You missed it!' I kept telling him over and over in my mind. 'It was an earthquake! A really big one. Under our feet! And you missed it!'

The roaring noise that was so deafening had given way to eerie silence. The soothing rumble of the plant machinery was gone. No birds sang. Even that slight hum from the underwater stream we'd heard the night before had vanished. We sat there quietly, staring at the damage – the crumpled walls, the massive roof upended to the sky, great heavy doors spat out across the compound, with fallen rocks and mangled metal everywhere.

It was Dad who spoke first. 'So,' he said drily, 'Old Mother Nature has well and truly crapped on the carpet now.'

How cool was that? Sometimes my dad is amazing.

Miles fell in with Dad's weird mood of relief. 'Yes, Phil. I very much doubt if we'll be all tidied up, with everything properly serviced, by Tuesday.'

I wondered if they were hysterical and told them sternly, 'We should be careful. There might be aftershocks.'

Dad said, 'Since when did you become such a persistent dispenser of earthquake-safety tips?' He tried to scramble to his feet but, with his legs still shaking too much to support him, had to sit down again. That's when I saw, even under his coating of fine dust, the blood drain from his face, and that strange tic of his mouth that I had only ever seen once before, when he was carrying Toby's coffin into the church, along with my uncles. Now he was staring at me as if I were a ghost, and I was certain I could tell what he was thinking: *I've lost one son, and I just very nearly lost the other.*

I tried to make a joke to snap him out of it. 'Good job Mum didn't see all that.'

He stared at me a little longer, then breathed again. The others waited quietly. I know they realised something was going on deep inside Dad, and good old Valentina more than likely guessed what.

Finally, she spoke. 'Let's stay here a few minutes more. Now that things seem to be settling, it's probably no more dangerous than anywhere else. In any case, we need to think about what to do next.'

Again, we sat in silence. I watched Valentina. Up until then, she'd seemed to take things in her stride, but she was clearly just as rattled as the rest of us. A muscle under her eye twitched horribly. Her hands were trembling and, though she's supposed to be about the same age as my dad, suddenly, even under the strange grey silt of dust, her face looked much, much older.

'Thank God it's only water we deal with here,' she said at last. 'Not gas, or nuclear power.'

That's when my dad threw up.

SIX

Just stop. Please stop.

While we were sitting there, I thought of Mum and how soon she'd find out about the earthquake. I've been on walking trips with her. (Only a day or so. I can't stand more.) I know that she tries not to check her phone until the evening, and disapproves of those in her group who do. I thought it was most likely she didn't yet know. And, if she did, would she have even remembered that Dad had told her we were heading east? Now that the worst of it was over, and I was pretty sure that we were safe, I thought it was a shame that no one, probably not even Will, or any of my mates at school, would yet know I'd been part of something so spectacular. And none of the staff who get to school dead early would realise because, rather than face our rather scary head to ask permission for three full days

off, my dad had chickened out and told the office people
I was sick.

So, it was possible that nobody, not even Mum,
was hearing the words, 'Reports are coming in...' and
thinking, *An early morning earthquake across on the far
east coast? But what about* Louie?

I glanced at Dad. Though he was busy rubbing
the shoulder he'd bashed against the door when we
were getting out, I could still tell his thoughts were
miles away. Was he, too, wondering when Mum
would hear the news? He'd know her walking trip
would end right there and then. And he would feel so
guilty about the danger I'd been in, even though no
one could pin the blame on him. You can't go round
predicting earthquakes any more than you can know
that someone's cycle ride down to the corner shop will
end in death.

And it was Mum herself who had so cheerily told
him, 'You'll have to take Louie with you.'

Accidents happen.

That made me think again about what Valentina
had just said. 'Thank God it's only water we deal
with here.' Small wonder she was looking so grim and
thoughtful. She was an engineer, and engineers are

hired to fix things in all sorts of industries. If this had been a different sort of pumping plant, what I'd been through might not have simply been extraordinary – something I'd never forget – it might have been a massive,fiery explosion that blew us all to bits. Or a nuclear disaster, to frizzle us more slowly.

Out of the four of us, I reckon it was Miles who pulled himself together first. Dusting his hands together, he pushed his hair back from his face. 'I'm parched. And starving. We can't sit here for ever. Let's close down what's left of the plant, and leave.'

'This plant has closed itself down,' Valentina pointed out.

'Then we'll just leave.'

Suddenly they all seemed more like their old selves. 'Right, then,' Dad said. This time he managed not just to struggle to his feet, but to stay upright. 'We'll have a quick look round to see if we can safely rescue any gear, and then we'll go.'

'Go where?' I asked.

'Home, of course. Back to civilization.'

'But how?'

He pointed to the van we'd travelled in. And it was only then that he appeared to see for the first time that not only had a heap of giant boulders from the ridge stoved in the front of it, but it was lying on its side.

I cannot tell you how unnerved I was to see Dad's face drop in the way it did. Up until then, I'd always thought of him as someone totally on top of things. Broken toys, flickering lights, dripping taps, blocked drains – Dad could sort anything. He would just stare at the problem for a while. ('The diagnosis', Mum called it.) He might say, 'Hmmm', or even, 'Now this might be a little tricky…' But he would still put everything to rights again. He even sorted his and Mum's separation out brilliantly. She openly admits that.

But there was going to be no fixing this. Even an engineering Know-Nothing like me could tell that straightaway.

I glanced at the other two, hoping that neither of them felt as crushed as I did. Miles was, I thought, eyeing Dad surreptitiously from under his mop of hair. But Valentina had turned her face upwards.

'Look!'

I tipped back my head and saw masses and masses of birds, all flying over us, all heading inland. I couldn't think what looked so odd about them until I realised they were not a proper flock. Up there were birds of every shape and size and speed of flight. It seemed that anything lucky enough to have wings had suddenly decided to get away from the coast.

Valentina muttered something.

'What?' I demanded.

She looked at me as if she hadn't realised that she'd spoken aloud.

'What was that you said?' I persisted. 'What are you thinking?'

The other two were watching Valentina as closely as I was now, wondering if she would tell me. At last, she said, 'The birds. I'm thinking…'

Again, she paused. So it was Miles who, in the end, came out with it.

'Tsunami?'

I turned to stare at him. 'A tidal wave? You're joking!'

'It's possible,' said Miles. 'Quite likely, actually.'

He said it almost as casually as if he were talking about a probable delay at some roadworks.

'But we'll be perfectly safe here,' Valentina assured me. 'Truly. Safer than anywhere.'

I was still panicking. 'But what about that pathway over the ridge? The one you thought the caretaker would use. Won't water get through there?'

She shook her head. 'No chance.'

I wasn't in the least convinced. 'You said it was an easy climb!'

'Not all that easy,' Valentina soothed. 'Believe me, Louie, however high the water rises, it won't get over the ridge.'

'Promise?' I begged. (I must have sounded four years old.)

'Promise,' she said.

Nobody spoke after that. I don't know what was running through their minds, but I was wondering how furious my mum was going to be when she learned how much danger I'd been in, even if it wasn't Dad's fault. And then I wished that Toby was beside me, sharing it all, not just because his being there had always made me feel safer, but also because, ever since Toby died, each time that something's happened that I know my brother would have hated to have missed, it's also spoiled for me. I don't like going swimming on Saturday mornings now. I only go to films with Will so I can join in people's arguments about them at school. And I won't even go on fair rides any longer. All of the things Toby and I used to do together are ruined now that the only thing that I can think of all the way through is his not being there, and all I can feel is the business of missing him. And though sitting waiting for a natural disaster isn't a swimming session or a film or a fair ride, I still was desperate for Toby to be there.

I was distracted by Valentina, noticing that she kept leaning towards Dad to read the time on his old-fashioned watch. 'Are we still waiting to see if there's to be a tidal wave?' I asked. 'There'll be an early warning system, surely. Wouldn't we have heard it by now?'

'Possibly not,' she admitted. 'The gauges might be too far out. When a wave passes through a bay like this, it has a bigger impact. Or, if the detector buoys have been damaged by fishing nets—'

I didn't need another lecture. 'But surely the *earthquake* would have set off the alarm?'

'It should have done. But if the damage to the power lines is bad enough, sirens stop working. And if the cell phone towers come down, no automatic text warnings will get through either.'

It didn't sound too good. 'So how soon will we know?'

Dad said, 'I rather think we know already, Louie.' And that was when I realised it was no longer quiet all around. Now I could hear what sounded like a rising wind. Valentina and Dad exchanged glances, and I finally cottoned on that all the time I had been sitting there, the two of them – and probably Miles as well – had in their minds an ever-widening lip of water drawing back the whole length of this bay I'd never seen, sucking back slowly and steadily into itself, and rising higher and higher into a vast, curved, slippery wall of water, while more and more of all that previously hidden ocean floor gleamed in the morning sunlight for the first time ever.

They had, I realised, known from the moment the earthquake started that this might happen.

'Nine minutes,' Dad said. 'Maybe a little more.'

Nine minutes. Was that *all*? More to the point, if it were just nine minutes since the earthquake, then was that good? Or really bad? It didn't mean a thing to me until Miles muttered, 'Big one...'

'Those poor, poor people,' whispered Valentina, making me realise that, just as I count the seconds between a lightning flash and the first clap of thunder to work out the distance of a storm, these three had inwardly been counting the minutes to this new sound of rushing wind, unable to keep themselves from trying to estimate how bad this tidal wave was likely to be.

And then it struck me that the noise bearing down on us might not be wind at all. Not wind, but water – a massive, gathered bank of water now hurtling towards the shore. Unstoppable. And there was nothing to do but sit there, trying to block my ears against the penetrating din. Who would have thought that water spreading across land the far side of a ridge could make a noise like that? Louder and louder it grew, until it sounded like a thousand waterfalls falling as one. I knew the wall of water would stretch in both directions as far as the eye could see, and further. What was to slow it now? Shutting my eyes, I saw it creeping places it had never reached before, first in frilled runnels snaking their way up the beach between the boats that had been dragged above the highest tide line, then, as the weight of water behind pushed, pushed and pushed, thundering up to the huts in which the fishermen kept their nets and tackle, devouring them in an instant and crashing on between the scrubby trees, foaming across the beach road to swirl around, swamping the houses on the other side and ripping them from their foundations. Oh, I might never have seen the bay we were all thinking about, but as that great rush of noise stopped sounding either like wind or water, and more like metal being torn to shreds, it was too easy to imagine what was happening.

Now Miles had curled himself so far over his knees, his face was hidden. Dad was still staring at his watch face. Valentina was expressionless.

I saw Dad's lips move. I think that he was whispering, 'Just stop. Please *stop,*' over and over again. But still the noise got louder, till I could almost see the bodies tossed like cloth dolls, and house walls caving in as easily as if they'd been made from paper. I saw the fishing boats swallowed, cars bobbing like small corks on the black flood, trees splintering to matchsticks.

'Stop it!' I echoed Dad. 'Just stop it! *Please!*'

And, after what seemed an age, the noise did start to falter, and then ease. I took my hands from over my ears and wiped away the tears I hadn't realised were the reason why everything around me had turned into a burning kaleidoscope.

We sat and looked at one another – Dad, Valentina, Miles and me.

All perfectly safe, as Valentina had promised.

SEVEN

Over the ridge

'Phones,' Dad said. (He was back on top of things.) 'We should tell Swati just how bad things are. I know I left mine in there by the sleeping mat. Louie, where's yours?'

'On top of the backpack you told me I should leave behind.'

'I hope that's not a criticism,' Dad responded sharply. He pointed to what was left of the pumping station. 'I will remind you how fast we had to get out of there.'

Valentina stepped in. 'Mine's in the pocket of my jeans.' She nodded towards the mess. 'Somewhere in there.'

'I left mine in the van,' said Miles. 'Let's try that first.'

We brushed ourselves off a bit, then gathered round the overturned van. Miles clambered up and tugged at one of its doors. 'Totally jammed.'

'Try the other.'

Cautiously, Miles stepped back and reached down to tug at the handle. From where I was standing, that door looked even more battered, but, 'Bingo!' said Miles, and lowered himself inside.

Dad and Valentina used a broken length of pipe to jemmy open the van's back doors and prop up one side while Valentina pulled out a heap of overalls, the work boots all of them had tossed in before the journey, and the old pair of climbing boots Dad had bunged in for me.

Now and again, Miles's head popped up and he threw something out to me. Half-empty bottles of water from the day before. A sweatshirt of Valentina's. One or two odd-looking tools. Packets of biscuits.

'Just stick to looking for your phone,' Dad told him. 'We can start the salvage work later.'

Valentina was sorting through work boots. 'Mine,' she said, holding up a pair. 'And with a sock balled up in one. No, *two* socks! Aren't I the lucky one?'

While she and Dad were clambering into overalls,

I rooted through to find something warm for myself. But even after I'd pulled on a grubby boiler suit and folded up the over-long legs on it, Miles still hadn't found his phone.

Dad got impatient. 'Come on. Let's leave him to it.'

We set off across the compound to look more closely at what was left of the building. What a mess! So much had been destroyed. Dust was still settling, and each time there was a tiny tremble underfoot, small clouds of dust puffed off the ground and shivered in the air.

'Stay clear! Stay back!' The way that Dad kept tabs on me, you would have thought he reckoned I was daft enough to dive headlong into the wreckage. He wouldn't let me move more than an arm's length away, and every time I tried to shake him off, he muttered, 'Aftershocks,' and pulled me back.

Odd things were lying all around, hurled out by the quake. The portable cooler Miles had been so proud of stocking with goodies lay halfway across the compound, face down in the dust. Crushed lengths of pipe and buckled strips of metal were scattered all over. A massive boiler I didn't even remember seeing on the walk round the pumping station the night before had been torn from its base. It was still rocking gently, hissing in angry spurts as if it was wondering whether or not to bother to topple over completely and make even more mess. Not far away, shiny black slicks from a gashed oil tank were dribbling this way and that.

We rounded what was left of the corner of the building to see that the area in which we'd spent the night was flattened. The outer wall had caved in totally, and chunks of jagged roof lay on the top.

'Hopeless,' Dad told me. 'Step away.'

'There's nothing left to fall,' I argued.

'This is an *earthquake* we're dealing with,' he snapped. 'Aftershocks hurl things upwards almost as often as they fetch them down.'

Valentina was weighing up the damage further along, trying to work out exactly where in the chaos we'd all been sleeping. 'I reckon my mat must have been behind that mangled ventilation shaft.'

I stood there, rather hoping I would hear Dad saying, 'Hmmm,' or, 'That might be tricky . . .' as usual. But no such luck. He simply shook his head. 'It's a lost cause, trying to find anything useful in there. Thank God the work boots were in the van. Without them, it would have been no picnic, getting over the ridge.'

'Is that where we're going?' I asked him. 'Over to the bay?'

'No choice,' he said. 'How else can we get out of here? Even if we could manage to lever the van upright again, and get it started—'

'Which isn't possible,' said Valentina.

'— the road out has to be impassable now.'

Just then, across the compound, Miles's head popped up again. 'Found it!'

'Thank God for that!' Dad muttered. 'Oh, thank God for that.'

We hurried back.

'No signal, though,' warned Miles.

I watched Dad's face. He didn't look the slightest bit surprised, or even worried. 'But it is working?'

Miles rubbed dust off the phone and took a longer look. 'I think so. Yes, I'm pretty sure.'

'Then we'll get off.'

Miles, it turned out, had kept his trainers on all night. 'My feet were frozen.'

'Wear your boots anyway,' insisted Dad. Valentina passed him his overalls and he clambered into them. Stringing his trainers together by the laces, he slung them round his neck.

Dad looked us up and down. 'Ready, troops?'

We did, in fact, look like a proper team, all dressed in the same faded blue.

'What are we taking with us?' Valentina asked.

Miles opened a canvas bag to show her the water bottles and the biscuits.

'Your little cooler survived,' I told him, pointing. 'Almost.'

In a flash, he was striding towards it.

Valentina said to Dad, 'Are we not taking any tools?'

'My plan,' said Dad, 'was just to climb the ridge as quickly as we can, hopefully find a phone signal, and take a look at the bay. Then we can all agree on what to do next.'

'You hope,' said Valentina.

He gave her a puzzled look. 'Meaning?'

'Meaning,' said Valentina, 'that we can go up there and see what's what. But whether we'll all agree on what to do next is quite a different matter.'

EIGHT

Is this for real?

There is a strange sort of relief in getting out of danger.
It makes you more light-hearted than before. I know I
wasn't the only one to feel that way as we set off along
the badly fractured road to find the path over the ridge.
I heard Miles whistling to himself under his breath,
and, almost as if the two of us were on a normal Sunday
morning walk, Dad pointed out odd things – a colourful
snake that hung, dead, over one of the many viciously
split branches, a rock that looked a bit like a chef's hat,
even a tortoise helpless on its back. (We put it right and
watched it as it plodded off to disappear under a clump
of grey lichen balled up against one of the uprooted
trees.)

We found the caretaker's bike lying as carelessly
abandoned as it had seemed the night before, outside the

compound. I turned towards the ridge and looked for the path we knew he must have followed. And it was clear enough – a narrow trodden track between waist-high grasses. Not even all that steep; it looped up like a sheep's path on a hill.

'Right. Up we go.'

We went in single file because it was easier. Only occasionally did Dad or Valentina have to stop to catch breath, or take a moment's rest. It took less time than I expected; not far ahead, the pathway opened up into a flattish gully between two knuckles of the ridge.

I heard Miles calling from the back. 'Hey, can you all stop for a moment?'

I got the feeling Dad was ready to ignore him, but Valentina tapped Dad on the back. 'Hang on, Phil. Miles wants to take a break.'

Dad turned. We could all see that Miles was rummaging in his canvas bag. First, he pulled out a packet I assumed must be the biscuits he had rescued from the van. Then he pulled out a wide-mouthed Thermos flask.

'So, what's in there?' I asked, as he unscrewed the top.

'Ice cream.'

'*Ice cream?* Up *here?* Right *now?*'

He seemed surprised that I had any doubts. 'A perfect time for it, surely, after that climb? If we don't eat it now, it's going to turn to mush. No point in wasting it.'

And in a way, it did make sense. We'd eaten nothing since the night before. So I sat on a flattish patch of rock nearby, and waited.

Miles hadn't simply brought the flask. In the fat packet I'd assumed was biscuits, he carried sugar cones. He even had a metal spoon. 'How come?'

'I bunged it in the packet.'

Scooping a massive dollop of vanilla ice cream on to a cone, he handed it to me. 'There you go. Breakfast.'

The sun was up, and I was warm from the climb – and very hungry. 'Thanks.'

He filled a cone for Valentina, and one for Dad. I could tell from their faces that they thought ice cream an odd thing to eat right then and there, but neither of them said so. By then, we were in easy reach of the gap to take us over the ridge, so we kept walking. But there was something about eating ice cream in warm sunshine on a flattish stretch of track that made us slow our pace. We idled up the slight slope to the highest part of the walk. I lowered my eyes to lick the drips from round the rim of my cone, and found myself stumbling against Dad's back.

He'd stopped dead. So, I realised, had Miles and Valentina. The three of them stood silently in a line.

I stepped up beside them to find out what they were staring at.

And then I saw. It hit me, almost like a punch in the gut. I thought that we'd seen devastation on our side. The pumping station, after all, was no more than a heap of rubble now, walls down, roof torn off, all equipment ruined. But this was chaos of a different kind. I thought I had imagined something bad enough, but in my mind's eye there'd been nothing – *nothing* – to match this. The view from the ridge was so entirely shocking it took a bit of time to work out what we were looking at down there. The world in front of us lay in three starkly different bands, each running off to either side as far as the eye could see. Furthest away there was the ocean itself, perfectly peaceful and calm, and shimmering silver in the morning light. Close to us, almost underneath our feet as we gazed down, there was a narrow strip of forest. Green. Perfect. Untouched.

But, in between, there lay a panorama of destruction. 'What *is* all that?'

The tidal wave had scattered everything. It had tossed trees about like matchsticks. Bits of smashed boats lay everywhere. The prow end of one was sticking out of what was left of someone's upstairs window. The back end of another was beached up on a mangled roof. I saw a shed upended in the broken branches of a tree. And then another. Not one post stood upright. Odd bits of house were floating here and there. Snapped planks of sodden wood lapped around everything, and all around were sprawled lengths of twisted wires, some spitting sparks in spite of all the water.

And bodies. Scores of twisted bodies. Caught in the splintered trees, pinned under logs, snarled up in fishing nets. For a moment I thought someone was flashing a torch at us in search of help. But then I realised it was just the sun glinting against a snapped-off sheet of something shiny bobbing along on the water. Everywhere I looked, grey foam was flying about and giant curls of something that looked like black toffee were all over. 'Is that the tarmac peeled up from a *road*?' said Miles. 'Was there a *road* down there? Where has it *gone*?'

Like all of us, he stood and stared some more. 'Is this for *real*?'

And truly, it did seem impossible. I wouldn't have believed that even a bombing raid could cause a fraction of the damage we saw that morning. This tidal wave had swept in with such force it had uprooted everything and hurled it over and over, till it was smashed to bits.

Valentina was ashen. 'Sweet Jesus, what a *mess*!'

She meant what we were seeing in front of us. Of course she did. But I don't think Miles realised, because he suddenly held his melting ice cream further away from his blue overalls, as if to save them from the drips.

'Whoops!'

That's when we looked at one another properly, for the first time since we'd reached the top of the ridge. What were we *doing*, standing in a line, staring at utter destruction, scores of lost lives, and chaos and misery that never could be sorted. Never.

Just standing there like idle, rubber-necking tourists, holding our stupid ice creams.

NINE

Far too many memories

I know that by the time you're out of primary school, you're supposed to have stopped believing that your dad's the strongest, bravest person in the world. Still, I turned to him then the way I always had, supposing that he would know exactly what to say and what to do. But he looked blank. It wasn't shock or horror on his face. It wasn't anything I'd ever seen. It looked more like *defeat*, as if the things that he was staring at were all too much for him, and, like a piece of equipment that had fused, he'd just closed down. Watching Dad stand there, at the top of that ridge, with that strange look, triggered in me a feeling of real panic and, along with that, far too many memories – all of them bad.

Toby died on his birthday. He had been cycling only as far as the local shop, to get some icing sugar so Mum could finish his cake. We heard the sirens shrieking by on the main road, but none of us realised it was anything to do with Toby till the police car pulled up outside our house.

I look back, but the two weeks after that are mostly a blur. I can remember tripping over a dish that one of the neighbours had left on our doorstep, and feeling the warm, meaty sludge of the casserole inside spill on my sock. The awful wail my dad let out when my uncles lifted the wicker coffin back on to their shoulders at the end of the funeral service. My mother furiously sweeping the line of sympathy cards off the dresser and shouting, 'I cannot *look* at these a moment longer!'

Things never got back to normal. With Toby gone, how could they? It was as if the four of us had been in the middle of some complicated game of cards, and suddenly my brother had got up and walked out. We couldn't work out how to get things going again. Or even whether to try. Everything seemed pointless. And even though I knew that Mum and Dad were going through the very same feeling I had almost every minute – of missing Toby horribly – I still felt dreadfully alone. I'd wake in the morning and – *boof!* – the fact that he was dead and gone would hit me again. I'd see some pencil he'd chewed, or one of those lemon curd tarts he had a passion for, and – *boof!* – over and over, because I'd keep forgetting. A thousand times a day I told myself, 'I must remember to tell Toby this,' or, 'That will give Toby a laugh.' Once, when my mum and dad were out, I even went into the hall and shouted, '*To*-bee!' up the stairs because it seemed so long since I'd been able to call out like that.

I know that Mum and Dad were miserable too. Mum couldn't even go in Toby's room. It stayed the way it was. Nobody stripped the bed, or tidied up. Whenever I was in the house, both of them acted as if the room didn't exist. The door stayed shut, and they walked past. Sometimes I wondered if, while I was out at school, one or other of them ever crept in to sit on his crumpled bed and look around at all his stuff. But I don't think so. Both of them seemed to me to be barely holding themselves together. They picked their way round one another with weird, tiny politenesses they'd never used before.

'Anna, would you be comfier with a cushion?'

'There is a bit more pie, Phil, if you would like it.'

But neither of them even began to act the way they usually did with one another.

Until Mum's outburst.

A friend from work had brought a bag of chocolate brownies with her when she came to see how Mum was coping. I'd snaffled quite a few already, but there were several left, and I was hanging around the kitchen hoping that, rather than going to the bother of putting them away, Mum wouldn't mind me polishing off the rest. It didn't look as if I was in luck because she was scrabbling around in cupboards, looking for something to store them in. But all the usual containers were in the freezer, filled with the food that people had been bringing round for us.

Mum moved to one of the other cabinets and, without thinking, fetched out the yellow cake tin and flipped off the lid. Inside was Toby's birthday cake – the one that had been waiting to be iced.

The blood drained from her face. 'Oh, *Jesus!*'

'Here, give it me,' I said. 'I'll throw it out.'

She pushed the tin towards me as if it had been filled with snakes. I took it outside to the wheelie bin. First, I just tipped in the cake. But then I realised Mum would never, ever want to see that yellow tin again. So I dumped that as well.

When I got back in the house, Dad had come into

the kitchen and Mum was brushing away tears. 'Oh, well!' she said bitterly. 'At least, with Toby being killed on his birthday, we only have one date in the year, not two, when we'll have to feel even more wretched.'

'Now, there's my Anna,' Dad said. 'As thrifty as usual, even in grief.'

I know he meant it as a sort-of joke, trying to pick up and run with what Mum herself had said. And I am pretty sure she knew that, too. But it was as if she suddenly decided to use his words as an excuse to let rip. Instantly, she was shouting.

'How dare you? How *dare* you? Can you imagine, for a single moment, that even a *minute* goes by without that boy being on my mind? My first thought when I wake! My last thoughts when I'm trying – trying!– to get to sleep! For every minute of every endless, pointless day! Whatever I'm doing and wherever I am! He haunts my every waking hour and most of my bloody dreams! How *dare* you try to imply that I'm not grieving for him?'

I could tell Dad was panicking. 'Hey, come on, Anna! That's not what I said and it's not what I meant, and you know that!'

'I don't know anything!' she wailed. She dropped on

61

to a chair and laid her head on the table. Her voice came out all muffled. 'I don't even know how to get through my days! All I know is that Toby is right beside me, all the time. I know exactly what he would be saying. I know the look that would be on his face. He might as well be bloody *here* with us, he is so real to me. So absolutely here! And I can't stand it! It is driving me *insane.*'

She cried for hours. Dad had to almost carry her up to bed. He shut their door on me, but I could hear her sobbing, even from my room. Next day, she walked around like someone in a daze till Dad, who had gone back to work, came home and packed her off to bed again.

When he came down, I asked him, 'Will she be all right?'

'She has no choice,' he said. 'None of us do, really, do we?'

TEN

Something bad on its way

What Dad said then came back to me, up on that ridge. Had he, too, just been ploughing on, thinking he had no choice? And could this awful scene in front of us have just been one horrific thing too many – enough to make him feel he could no longer carry on dealing with things, the way that adults do. After all, Mum had admitted she didn't know how to get through her days. But we all knew she had to keep on trying because of me. *I* was still there. If she'd just given up completely, what sort of message would that have sent to me? 'I'm afraid you don't count for as much as your brother'? That isn't very nice.

And even in my darkest moments, I never thought it was true. I knew that if it had been me who had been cycling off to buy that icing sugar at the exact wrong time, and had got killed, she would be just the same, and Toby would have been as helpless as I was, not knowing what to do or what to say. Just standing, like a dummy, waiting for time to pass and Mum to turn back into Mum.

Dad loves me too. So, though the dead look on his face had frightened me, I knew he'd shake the demons off, and get a grip. After all, Mum had managed. The long days had crawled by, but when her boss rang up to offer her another three weeks' leave, she'd said she'd rather be at work. She'd started back the next day, and I was pleased for her. I know I'd felt a whole lot better when I was in school.

At first, that had been pretty bad. I'd kept my eyes firmly ahead as I walked through the gates, but I could sense that everyone around was stepping back, and whispering and staring. I almost turned and fled but, as I was dithering, Will Hutchins stepped up. 'Our team is going to get *mashed* without your brother.'

And that is Will all over. I don't know how he always manages to say the right thing in the right way, but somehow the tension broke. People came up to me. Some said how sorry they were. Some patted my back as they walked past. Aoife had a little silver squirrel her mother had told her to give me 'as a comfort in your loss'. Before lunch, I was asked to go along and see Ms Dale, the counsellor, but it was obvious to both of us the session didn't go well. Ms Dale looked anxious about that, but how could I tell her that the only person in the world I might have wanted to talk to about my brother's death was my dead brother? I couldn't. One of the things she asked was if I wanted other people in school to talk to me about it all, or not. And I chose not, so school would turn into a sort of break from missing Toby. And though it was quite obvious that Ms Dale didn't think I'd made the right choice, and seemed a little sorry she'd given me the option in the first place, I stuck to my guns.

That wasn't quite the end of the session. She sat there, eyeing me for a while over her steepled fingers, and then she said, 'But, Louie, are you getting any other help?'

'Other help?'

'Talking to someone. Have your parents managed to arrange for you to see a counsellor out of school about all this?'

'Oh, yes,' I lied to her. 'They've managed that.'

'And how's it going?'

'Fine,' I said. But when the look on her face made it quite clear I'd not been all that convincing, I laid it on thicker. 'It's very helpful. I thought that talking about it, especially to someone who didn't know him, would only make things worse. But it helps a lot. Really.'

'That's good,' she said. And though I knew she hadn't actually crossed me off the list of people in the school she had to worry about, I reckoned I was off the hook, and I was glad about that.

So things had been getting that bit easier for all of us when the police rang. Dad took the message because Mum never picked up the phone any more. She let the landline ring until it went to answerphone, and even then she left the room so she'd not hear the stumbling messages of sympathy that were still dribbling in. 'Just listen and delete them, Phil. I only want to know who's rung.'

That meant that it was Dad who picked up the police request to phone them back. As usual, I was eavesdropping, but couldn't work out what it was about. Dad seemed to mostly be saying, 'Oh, I see,' and, 'Thank you for letting us know,' over and over. He put the phone down and went off to look for Mum.

She was pulling his damp blue work overalls out

of the washing machine. I stayed behind the door and out of sight, so I could listen. 'That was the police,' said Dad. 'They had a message from the hospital about James Harper.'

My stomach clenched. James Harper was the boy who had been driving the car that killed my brother. He hadn't passed his test, it wasn't his car and he had no insurance. After he drove into Toby, he lost control and the car spun into a brick wall. He wasn't wearing a seat belt, and he had been in hospital ever since.

I could tell from Mum's voice that she had straightened up and turned around. 'Yes? What about him?'

'It seems that yesterday his parents agreed to switch off his life support.'

I hadn't realised that he was on life support. I had been thinking of James Harper as getting better every day.

There was a long, long pause, and then Dad added, just to make things clear, 'So, now he's dead.'

'Good!' Mum said fiercely. 'Good! I am very glad. I couldn't be more pleased.'

I wondered if my dad would dare to argue with her. One of Mum's friends had made the serious mistake a few days earlier of saying something sympathetic about how James Harper was only a year or so older than Toby himself, and that the accident would have a terrible effect on his young life. Mum practically shoved her out of the door, and wouldn't answer any of the messages from her that came in afterwards. Dad had to slip round to the woman's house to warn her to back off.

But Dad said nothing to Mum. He just turned to walk out, and caught me in the shadow of the door. 'Did you hear that?'

I didn't know whether he meant the news about James Harper, or what Mum said, or both. I told him, 'Yes, I heard,' but didn't add that I was just as glad as Mum. Right from the moment when the news came in that Toby was dead, I had been hating James Harper. I had been hating him so hard I sometimes found my hands were cramping with the urge to strangle him. Before I even knew his name I had been planning to track him down when he got out of hospital and pay him back in the worst ways I could imagine. I had worked out a hundred different schemes. It was the only thing that I could think about in bed at night.

So, I was as fiercely pleased as Mum to hear the

stupid, dangerous little weasel was stone-cold dead without any help from me. I would be free from wasting my own sleepless hours in hating him. Maybe I could, I thought, get halfway back to normal myself.

And I was right. The news about James Harper did make things easier. Instead of lying in my bed, stewing about that toerag, I could let thoughts of my brother drift through my mind. And I don't know whether it was because of what my mother had said about Toby still being there for her every minute of the day, and knowing what expression would be on his face, and what he would have said. But now that I'd stopped planning horrible revenges on James Harper, I too found myself free to start imaginary conversations with my brother. I told him what I thought was going wrong between Mum and Dad. I told him about the fact that neither of them ever seemed to go into his room. I even told him about two of the people at school who were driving me mad by being too sympathetic, looking at me with dewy eyes in the corridors, and practically cooing over me. And that, I told him, brought the whole horrid business straight back to mind in the only place where I was managing, most of the time, to put it aside. ('Don't say a thing,' was his advice. 'They're making a meal of it more for themselves than for you. Make some excuse to rush away, and leave them to wallow.')

I'd lie in bed each night remembering the good and bad things he and I had shared over the years. The two brilliant holidays in Italy. The dreary week we spent in that smelly caravan in Elgin. The way he stuck up for me in the playground when we were both in primary school. The time he'd given me his big fat china piggy bank when I'd smashed mine. Things like that. I'd not forgotten that we'd had some epic rows, and scores of little feuds and meannesses. But somehow, they had vanished into thin air. None of them mattered any more. In my mind, Toby had become a sort of teenage saint.

It's easy to suppose that people round you are following the very same path. At first, I just assumed Mum must be dealing with things better now too. After all, weeks had gone past. She had bad moments, of course. The time she hurled the second packet of hamburgers back in the supermarket freezer chest, howling, 'When am I *ever* going to remember I'm only shopping for *three*?' (The shoppers round us stared.) The time the vicar hurried to cut her off after she'd crossed the road to avoid him, and tried to talk to her about Toby. '"Safe in the arms of Jesus", indeed!' Mum told us after. She was still shaking with rage. 'I very nearly punched him!'

Times like that.

But it was quite a while before I really noticed that her behaviour was still odd with us. She was super-polite and careful with Dad. Things she would usually have lost her rag about – old tissues in the pockets of trousers he'd dumped in the laundry basket, milk cartons left out to sour overnight – she just passed over, or she mentioned them so gently you'd think it was the first time Dad made that mistake. It was as if she wanted her behaviour to be perfect. Beyond reproach. At first, I thought she must be in a muzzy cloud of grief, and taking a fake-it-until-you-make-it approach to picking her way through the days.

Then she exploded.

Dad had been clearing out the cupboard under the stairs, pulling out heaps of things and piling them behind him, all the while asking Mum, 'Do we still need this?', and, 'Surely there must be a better place for us to keep these?'

She kept her patience. But then Dad called, 'What shall I do with these?'

'With what?' she called back.

'These.'

I looked up. Dad was holding out a pair of Toby's running shoes. They were brand new. If Toby had even worn them twice, I'd be surprised.

There was one of those awful, awful silences when you just know that something bad is on its way.

'You can't even say his name, can you?' Her voice was icy with scorn. 'He was your son, and you can't even say his name aloud. You never mention him, and if I do, you wriggle and squirm, and hope that I'll shut up. You try to go around as if he was never here. You act as if you would *prefer* that.'

'Anna—'

'No, don't "Anna" me, Phil! I have had enough. You've tried to cast your It-Never-Happened spell on everyone, and now even Louie here knows better than to say his brother's name when you're around.'

That shook me. Till my mum flung that at Dad, I hadn't realised. But it was true. If Dad was anywhere around, I never mentioned Toby.

'He lived *here*,' Mum said, flinging out her arms. Her voice rose. 'With us! In this house! He was in every corner of it, day after day, from the first week he was born. Not one square inch of it is free of him. How can you even *begin* to want to try to pretend he isn't part of us? How can you *do* that?'

Dad tried again. 'Anna, be fair! We all have different ways of trying to deal with things like this, and—'

She cut right in on him. 'Things like this? *Things like this?* What are you *talking* about? There *is* nothing like this! Nothing! This is the very *worst*.'

He tried to reach for her. She pushed him away. 'No! Do it your way, if you must! But don't think for a minute that banning the name "Toby" from this house does you, or any of us, any favours!'

'I *never* banned the word. I just can't— Just can't—'

Dad stopped. His face was set. I waited. Nothing else was said. After a moment or two, Dad turned back to the cupboard he was clearing, and Mum went outside 'for a breath of air'.

But it was on the following day that she went looking for another place.

ELEVEN

Treading on eggshells

So that was where I was dropped after I'd been evacuated from the bay. It had been quite a journey, and when the driver sent by Dad's firm to pick me up at the small military airport in Sachard wanted to check where we were going, I was so tired I nearly gave him the address of our old house, rather than Mum's new flat.

Though she'd been there for weeks by then, both of my parents still talked as if it was a temporary arrangement. (*Good luck with that,* said Toby in our imaginary chat one night.) And I was hopeful. Mum and Dad had made no formal arrangements. Nobody talked of proper, legal divorce. From what I gathered, pretty well all their friends and colleagues were advising both of them to think of it as a short break from one another 'while things are settling down'. I think most of them thought that Mum was making her decisions far too soon, and that, if he lost hope, my dad would fall to pieces.

They both apologised to me for the upheaval. But I admit they did seem better apart. There was less of that treading on eggshells stuff that had made all of us so tense. Nothing in Mum's routine changed much, but when I was with Dad he tried to take time off, or get home early. My maths improved because it was mostly him now, and not her, who sat beside me explaining the reasons for things and doing it a good deal better than she ever had because her only aim was getting me to the right answer as fast as possible so we'd be finished. And there were other things that Mum had always done that Dad began to enjoy. He had to do a lot more cooking than before, and took more chances than Mum ever had with strange ingredients. ('What's this weird-looking stuff? Bung a bunch in the trolley, Louie. We'll look it up when we get home.') Together, we became dab hands at cooking Indian, Malaysian and Chinese dishes. And now, of course, Dad had to drive me to a lot more sports practices and matches. Instead of going home, as Mum had always done for the two hours in between drop off and pick up, he joined the sports centre gym, and even took a diving class for adults.

'Hoping to meet someone?' I teased.

That didn't go down well. 'I love your mother,' he told me sharply. 'I always have done and I always will.'

'Okay, okay. Keep your hair on.'

He pulled himself together and made a joke of it. 'I think we should simply think of this new membership card as my way of keeping in shape for when your mum's ready to come back.'

Next time that I was at her place, I told her what he'd said, adding, 'You know he *wants* you to come back. He really does. So *will* you?'

'Maybe.' She shrugged. 'And maybe not. We'll see.'

As my imaginary Toby reminded me in bed that night, when it came to our mum, 'we'll see' would usually end up meaning, 'no'. But she, too, did seem happier. At first, I'd rather dreaded my days at the tiny ground floor flat she'd rented on the far side of the park. I had assumed, after that outburst over the running shoes, that she would want to talk about Toby all the time. Let it out, safely away from tight-lipped, grieving Dad. But I was wrong. Toby's name came up. ('If you need money for school, why don't you have the sense to ask me the night before? Your brother was never daft enough to leave things like this until morning.' 'This omelette is perfect, Louie. Well done! Do you remember those leathery slabs of burnt egg that Toby used to produce? God, they were frightful.') But mostly she was more her normal self. She rejoined her walking club. She volunteered at the nearby homeless shelter. And she had streaks put through her mousy hair.

After a month or two, I'd reached the stage where I was perfectly at home in either house. I had a heap of stuff in both. I took their messages about lost sports gear and school parents' evenings back and forth. ('Tell her I *know* those boots aren't here. She'll have to look again. And in her car.' 'Wednesday is best for me. But if your dad can't make that, tell him to let me know so I can switch things round. I'd much prefer that he and I spoke to your teachers together.')

A perfectly normal routine. So, when the driver drew up at the kerb outside Mum's flat, I was quite startled when she shot outside to hug me, squeezing me so hard I almost burst. She turned to the driver, saying, 'Oh, thank you! Thank you!' so often that you would have thought he was the helicopter pilot who'd flown me out of the disaster area.

She couldn't stop hugging me. 'Thank God you're back! I have been phoning your dad's boss every few hours. Until last night he kept on telling me there was no chance of getting either of you out of there for over a week.'

'I was dead lucky,' I explained. 'Dad managed to convince some army officer I was away from medication. And she gave one of her helicopter pilots the nod to take me back to base.' While Mum was still pleased and relieved to see me, I slipped in what I thought was the bad news. 'But someone who sorted out the travel from there to Sachard says that we'll have to pay for it. He found me a seat. But I'm to tell you that a bill for that will definitely come in.'

Mum didn't seem to have noticed what I'd said. 'But what about your dad?'

'He's still there. The helicopters were too busy flying out people who needed treatment to make room for him or Miles and Valentina.'

I didn't mention that none of them had even asked for seats. Even before the helicopter I was leaving on took off, they'd gone along the beach to help knock up something to do with safer drinking water. When he was hugging me goodbye, I'd asked Dad, '*Sure* you're not coming?', and he had given me a look as if to say, *Oh, Louie. See what's around you? Use your brain.*

It had been Valentina who had said, 'Louie, the three of us are *engineers*. And what do these people need?'

I didn't bother to say, 'Engineers.' I just hugged Dad again, and said goodbye, glad that the strange, defeated look I'd seen before was gone, and he was back to his old we-can-fix-this self. Miles, I thought, looked a bit down in the mouth at the idea of having to stay put in all that misery and mess and chaos. But, I supposed, if you're one of a team like that, you'd look pathetic – and a heel – if you just said you wanted to go home.

But I was certainly glad to be back, and treated like a hero by my mates for simply having been in such a place at such a time. They'd all seen what had happened on the news, so it was the helicopter ride that most of them envied. I'm sure the staff sussed out that Dad had spun a line about my being sick. But no one mentioned that, and since I'd only missed a couple of days, it only took a bit of catching up of homework before Mum and I fell back into our routine.

Dad stayed in touch, but it was a couple of weeks before he actually showed up again. Mum was quite startled to open the door to a knock and find him on the step.

'Surprise!'

She let him in. 'Surprise, indeed! Why didn't you let us know that you were on your way back?' Almost at once, as if remembering where he'd been and why he'd stayed away, she changed the question and her tone of voice. 'How *is* it out there now, Phil?'

Over a cup of tea, he told us. 'Things are still pretty grim. I'm glad we helped, though. I know we've been very useful. We managed to salvage enough equipment from the compound and the van to cobble together something that's set the survivors up with clean, safe water until their proper system is rebuilt, and we helped the response teams with lots of other jobs.'

'Why would the locals even want to stay?' Mum asked. 'We saw the footage on the news. Over and over. That place is *devastated*.'

'It's where they live,' Dad answered simply. 'Where they've always lived.'

'Even so…'

Dad shrugged. 'The thing is, Valentina was quite right about the people out there. She told us they were different.' He made an odd face. 'And they are.'

'What sort of different?' persisted Mum.

Dad looked uneasy. 'I don't know how to even start to explain. As if they're not quite of this world. They stand, so lank and pale and thin, and they are *watching* all the time. Staring. Not saying anything. Not arguing or discussing, just quietly *watching*. Then, after a while, you get the strangest feeling that their silence is a ploy to hide something.'

'What sort of thing?'

'So hard to say. Resolve, maybe? Simple defiance? Utter, utter stubbornness.'

I thought back to the pumping station caretaker, and how he had refused to show a flicker of response on that first night, but Mum looked puzzled.

'Okay,' Dad told her. 'Here's an example. A couple of quite important government officials were flown in pretty quickly. They offered all the people who'd survived a chance to pick up their lives again, further along the coast. Housing. Jobs. Starter grants. All manner of temptations. As far as I could tell, it was a pretty generous offer. And, looking round at what is left of the bay, you would have thought they'd all have jumped at it.' He gave a baffled shrug. 'But then,'

I tried to push him to finish. 'But then?'

He made a face. 'Their local representatives didn't respond. It was as if the very idea was such a non-starter they didn't even *hear* it. And here we are now, three weeks later, and they're *still* like that. Not even thinking about it. The ones that are left just keep on stubbornly mending their torn nets and fixing up their battered fishing boats as if...'

He stopped. There was a glitter in his eyes that looked like the start of tears.

Now it was Mum's turn to prompt him. 'Philip?'

He took a giant breath. 'As if so many of their children hadn't been swept away. As if more of their old folk had managed to clamber far enough up the ridge to be safe. As if the world they'd always had was still around them, somehow.' His voice turned husky and fierce. 'In fact, they act as if the whole disaster was just another of those bits of crappy luck that you expect in life, and they'd be best simply to soldier on, just as before.'

We were all quiet. I knew that both of them were thinking about Toby, and how the two of them had not quite managed to keep soldiering on, otherwise why would Dad be going back to our old house tonight, and Mum and I be staying in this flat?

I almost saw Mum push away her real thoughts.

Briskly, she said, 'Well, it was all a dreadful fright. Dreadful! Especially with Louie getting caught up in it all. But I suppose now, looking back on it, I'm glad the rest of you were there to help.'

Dad gave himself a little shake, as if to brush off a host of bad memories. 'We did our best,' he said. 'Together with the army personnel, we've knocked together a very passable first-aid clinic, and made enough of a school room for them to start again.' Here came another of those haunted pauses. 'That's if they're ever ready to face up to how few pupils there will be.' Seeing me watching, he made an effort to smile. 'I've even helped to mend a few boats. In fact, I've cobbled together so many make-and-mend bits of fishing tackle in the last couple of weeks that I reckon I'll be experienced enough to build an ark by the time I come back.'

'You *are* back,' Mum reminded him, adding, in the uneasy silence that followed, 'aren't you?'

Both of us watched him scrabble round for some good way of saying it. But in the end, he just came out with, 'No, Anna. I'll be going back.'

Mum's face set hard. 'Oh, yes? And when is that?'

He couldn't meet her eye. 'Soon,' he admitted. 'Very soon.'

Mum's voice was frosty. 'What does *that* mean, Phil?'

Now he was almost shuffling his feet on the carpet. 'Wednesday?'

'*This* Wednesday? Do you mean the day after tomorrow?'

He gave up trying to pretend he wasn't saying it. 'Yes. I suppose so. I have a seat back booked for early Wednesday morning.'

'You have a bloody cheek,' Mum snapped. 'You do have *family* here, you know.' Then, maybe because it struck her that it was she herself who'd weakened this particular argument by moving out, she chose to point at me, and tell Dad, 'This is the only son that you have left, if you remember. He *needs* you.'

You'd think she'd slapped him on the face, he looked so stricken.

I told Mum off. 'Bit harsh!' I said. 'If Dad wants to go back, he should. He has the skills they need, and I am not a baby.'

I could tell Dad was grateful for the support. 'And I am sorry, Louie. But I do have to do this.'

I hadn't wanted to take sides, and turn Mum's irritation on to me. But on the other hand, I felt quite proud to have a father who could do things, fix things, make things better for everyone along that hugely battered bay. Mum hadn't really seen it, the way that Dad and I had. But she must have quickly realised that trying to make him feel guilty was pointless, because she tried to steer the conversation down another path. 'But won't they want you back at work?'

'The firm is being more than reasonable,' Dad said. 'When we asked them for unpaid leave, they said they'd pay us for three months out there.'

Mum picked up on that at once. 'Three months!'

'I hope I won't be away that long.'

It was as if she hadn't heard. 'Your firm is paying three experienced employees to be away for all that time?'

'Two,' Dad admitted. 'Miles flew home with me, but isn't going back. And I'm not sure how long Valentina will stay.'

'So, it will mostly be Saint Philip out there, will it?'

Mum isn't usually sarcastic, so it was only then I realised how very angry she was.

TWELVE

Hi, Miles!

I never thought that Mum was mad at Dad for going back again because the responsibility of looking after me would fall on her. I knew she wasn't bothered about that. We got on perfectly well. (She'd always said that raising me was like a rest cure after raising Toby.) She made a point of telling me, after Dad left, that she'd been angry only because she felt I needed him around. *After all, you're already having to cope without your brother.*

I didn't tell her I'd got in the habit of conjuring Toby up almost whenever I wanted. I thought that would sound weird. So, I just said, 'I'm doing fine, Mum. Honestly. You needn't worry about me.'

And it was true. I missed my brother – yes, of course I did. I wished with all my heart the accident had never happened. I kept going back to that morning in my head over and over, wishing that Dad had thought to pick up icing sugar during the supermarket shop the day before, wishing that Toby had told Mum he was too old for a birthday cake with candles, and wanted pizza instead. I wished that Dad had called Toby back to shut the door behind him, or pass a screwdriver – anything to change the timing by a moment or two. I wished that Toby had bumped into his best mate, Jimmy St George, on the ride down the hill, and stopped for a chat about their swimming team's chances of winning the cup, or something about that week's homework.

Any one of those small, stupid possibilities, and Toby would still be alive. But I can't say that I was *miserable*. By then, my brother was no longer on my mind hour after hour. I was enjoying school more than I ever had. If I am honest, everyone was nicer to me after Toby's death, and Will and I were better mates than ever. And now I'd had the very rare experience of living through an earthquake and tsunami, I was quite popular. People who didn't even really know me had begun inviting me to things. I never had to spend my time alone unless I chose to.

So, there was no need for Mum to be so mad at Dad

on my account. And I could understand why he and Valentina wanted to stay and help. If all those people who'd survived were so determined not to move away from where they'd always spent their lives, what was the choice? Everything would have to be fixed. And once communications – or what passed for them – were up and running again, I spoke to Dad as often as I wanted. He sounded cheerful enough. He kept me up to speed with all the things he'd been doing. He told me he was missing me and Mum, and he and Valentina were absolutely sick of bunkhouse beds and lukewarm food. Still, they'd be staying for a little longer.

Mum happened to walk behind me as we were speaking, and she butted in. 'And what is "a little longer" likely to mean, Phil?'

You could tell that he squirmed at the question. 'I'm not quite sure yet, Anna.'

'Well,' she said, sweet as sugared poison. 'Make sure you let us know as soon as your period of Blessed Sainthood comes to an end.'

It was the very next Saturday that I bumped into Miles in town. The first I knew that something must be up was when he pretended not to have seen me. I spotted him on the far side of the road, waiting, like me, for the green crossing light. Then, when he noticed me and realised who I was, he spun round and walked off, fast.

Dead curious, I hurried after him. He walked so quickly we were almost at the next crossroad before I managed to get up beside him. 'Hi, Miles!'

He made as good a stab as possible of looking pleased to see me. 'Louie! Hey, great to bump into you! How are things?'

'Fine,' I said. 'Fine. Where are you off to?'

I knew that, to avoid me, he'd gone the other way from where he had been heading, so wasn't that surprised when he stared round, looking hunted, then ended up by saying, 'Nowhere in particular.'

I thought perhaps he was embarrassed that Dad and Valentina were still at the bay, and he'd copped out. Still, I could think of nothing to say except, 'Dad told us that you're home for good.' At this, he looked so horribly uneasy, I added out of sympathy, 'And I don't blame you.'

That startled him. But for the first time since I'd forced him to accept that I was there, he was the same Miles as before. 'I'm going to admit it,' he confessed. 'I couldn't wait to get away from that god-awful place.'

He gave a shudder. 'And nothing – nothing in the world – will ever get me to go back.'

I thought about the awful sight that met the four of us as we fanned out along the top of the ridge, stupidly licking our ice creams. Everything smashed up so badly you couldn't even guess what it had been. Those long and sodden half-empty flour sacks that turned out to be bodies. The wavy line of blackened, broken trash that ran the whole width of the bay and showed how high the tidal wave had reached in every place.

That's what I thought Miles had in mind. But I was wrong. He suddenly told me, with the most extraordinary force, 'The fact is, I don't know how your dad and Valentina can stand it – all that creepy stuff!'

'Creepy?'

'Well, what would *you* call it? All those strange things going on? And all those eerie, staring people who turn out not to even—'

He broke off. He had seen my baffled face. 'Your dad hasn't told you, has he?'

I said as casually as I could. 'Oh, yes. Of course he has.' But I could tell Miles knew that I was lying. He clammed up at once. 'Listen,' he said. 'It's really good to see you. I'm sure we'll bump into one another again. But right now, I'm already late for an appointment.'

I would have said, 'What happened to "nowhere in particular"?' but didn't get the chance.

Miles had already gone.

THIRTEEN

Spirits of Spite

I went home dead unnerved. Creepy stuff? *What* creepy stuff? Still, I didn't mention any of what Miles said to Mum. She'd finally come to terms with the fact that Dad had gone straight back to Causeway Bay. I didn't want to set her off again. But it was worrying. What had Miles meant? He had appeared quite frightened by it all.

I naturally asked Dad next time we spoke. We chatted for a while about what I'd been doing in school. (As usual, he had asked if I was working hard enough to do well in the coming exams.) He told me how the gangs of workers from the city were making steady progress repairing the narrow road along the bay, and other roads inland. 'I shall be glad never to have to get inside another helicopter in my life.' He told me

Valentina's husband kept nagging at her to come home.

And then I told him I'd bumped into Miles.

'Oh, yes? So where was that? In town?'

'Outside the Palace cinema. I saw him crossing at the lights.' I couldn't see the point in pussy-footing around, so got to the point. 'He said that really weird and creepy things are happening out where you are.'

'Miles said that?'

'Yes.'

I got the feeling Dad was playing for time while thinking fast. On the computer screen, he looked a little shifty. 'I wonder why he said that.'

'I wondered too.' I went on the attack. 'I would have asked him, but the moment he suspected you'd not said anything about it to me or Mum, he couldn't rush off fast enough.'

'Perhaps he was in a hurry,' Dad suggested weakly.

I splatted that idea. 'No. It was obvious he didn't want to talk about it.' I let the silence hang between us for a moment or two before I added, 'Just like *you*.'

Dad said defensively, 'I can assure you, I'm not hiding anything.'

I do hate being treated like a fool. And he's my Dad. I have the *right* to worry in case he's not safe. 'So why was Miles so surprised I didn't know about whatever it was that spooked him? If it was bad enough for him to rush home and claim that nothing in the world would ever drag him back?'

The trouble is, my saying that had given Dad the time to choose a line to try to fob me off. 'Just think about it, Louie. This place has been through the most awful experience. People are traumatized. They've lost their wives and husbands, grandparents, brothers and sisters – often even their children. They're in a shocking state. It's not at all surprising that some of them are massively sensitive, with their imaginations working overtime. You would expect this sort of—'

I interrupted all his flannelling. 'Do you mean that they're "seeing things"? Is that what you're trying to tell me?'

Dad suddenly sounded curt, almost ratty. 'I'm not "trying to tell" you anything, Louie. I'm simply explaining that, right now, some of the people here are not exactly sure about everything around them. So many ghastly things keep happening.'

'What sort of things?'

I know he didn't want to tell me. But in the end I suppose he thought it would be better to say something than nothing. 'Well, just to take one example, one of the things that wave did was lift out their burial ground.'

'Lift it out?'

'Well, *suck* it out. We didn't notice in all that chaos and mess. Why should we? We weren't familiar with the bay. But it turns out the locals had a graveyard up from the shoreline. That's where they kept their shrines.'

'*Shrines?*'

Dad still looked irritable. 'For heaven's sake, Louie. You surely know what a shrine is.'

'Of course I do. It's just that it sounds so…'

I broke off. The words that came to mind were 'foreign' and 'old-fashioned', and I didn't want to say either of those because someone tall and pale and hollow-cheeked – clearly a local – had just stepped into the frame.

Ignoring the figure behind him, Dad prompted me to finish. 'Go on. It sounds so – what?'

I realised then that Dad was wearing ear buds for the call. Whoever was behind him could hear every word he said. But unless Dad had also switched his laptop on to speaker phone, they couldn't hear me. Still, just in case, I took care to lower my voice. 'Old-fashioned, maybe?' I whispered.

Dad let out a ringing laugh. 'Louie, these people are *way* beyond old-fashioned. They're from another world. They have the most peculiar beliefs. They think, for example, that if anyone dies in the wrong way – too violently, or too soon – their spirit can't settle. And even if a long-buried body is disturbed, it can somehow call back a spirit that won't rest unless a living member of the family goes through some strange procedure. We could almost be talking about exorcism!'

'Dad,' I said softly, 'There's someone—'

He hadn't heard me. 'And if no living member or descendent of the family takes the time to go through this long, and horribly emotionally demanding, ritual they have, they truly do believe the spirit concerned will drift around unhappily for ever, causing mischief and scattering curses. They even have a name for them. They call them "Spirits of Spite".'

'Dad, I should tell you—'

But for a moment or two the picture pixilated and the sound broke up. He'd missed my interruption and, when things resolved, he was still busy speaking. 'You'd think that damage to an ancient burial ground would be the least of their problems. But they're so mired in their traditional patterns '

The elongated figure behind him was so blurred I couldn't clearly see the face. But I could certainly sense from the way the head was twisting round towards the screen that whoever it was wasn't taking too kindly to what my Dad was saying. Was it resentment that someone new to the Endlands was taking it upon himself to explain their ways? The look on the face now staring at the back of Dad's head appeared to me, even as out of focus as it was, to show a mix of indignation and rage.

Again, I tried to warn him. 'Da-ad!'

But he was on a hobby horse. It was the way he always starts to spout when anyone around him seems to be taking seriously things like astrology and fortune telling, or unscientific practices like homeopathy and 'healing with crystals'. He simply barged on. 'The problem is, these people are hindered by their need to respect all the old customs and beliefs. Right now, for example, most of them seem far more concerned with this strange ritual for placating unhappy spirits than with the practical things that this community needs most, like—'

'Dad! Dad!' I hissed, determined to interrupt him, but desperately hoping that only he could hear me.

'There's one of them behind you right now, listening to every word you say.'

He spun round to look. Then he turned back to me. 'Nice one, Louie. You really fooled me there. You nearly gave me a heart attack.'

The figure stared at me directly over Dad's shoulder and the screen went blank.

FOURTEEN

UncannyBay

Oh, it was creepy. Especially after what I'd heard from Miles. Not one of those things I could brush off as some stupid glitch in the system, or my imagination working overtime – or even, as I tried to tell myself, Dad seeing whoever was behind him perfectly clearly, then teasing me by saying what he did while surreptitiously pressing *End Call*.

No, I knew even then it was for real. I sat and worried about Dad for quite a while, but then I realised that, though Miles had claimed nothing could persuade him to go back himself, he would quite definitely have said if he thought either Dad or Valentina might be in danger. He'd not said anything like that. He'd simply made it clear he couldn't stand that sort of eerie stuff himself.

And I'm not all that brave. But Dad and Valentina were still there. How could it be that bad? And suddenly, all that I wanted was to go back again to Causeway Bay, and not to see the changes and improvements Dad and Valentina had made.

I wanted to go back to see the creepy stuff myself.

I wasn't going to tell Mum. No way. So, I just started on her sideways. 'When is your walking club's next trip?'

She shrugged. 'Some time in early July, but I won't be going.'

'Why not? You said you had a really good time on the last one – before Dad and I spoiled it by getting caught up in that stuff at the bay.'

'I'm sure I'd have a really good time again. But I have you to consider, don't I? I don't want to end up wasting a series of bed and breakfast deposits, with us still having no idea when your dad will be back.'

I pounced. 'I could go out to him, just for that week.'

She couldn't have looked more horrified if I'd suggested I spend the week sleeping in some backstreet skip. 'What? Back to that awful place? After everything you told me?'

'It's not that bad any more. I told you, Dad says the government has got its act together. The food's miles better, and he says he's sleeping in a fairly comfortable cabin. And they have lots of volunteers there. I could be one of them.'

She rolled her eyes at me, so I turned up the pressure. 'It would be after term ends.'

'True.'

I didn't think she'd buy the goody-goody, let-me-be-unselfish line, so I began the normal wheedling I'd do for anything else. 'Oh, come on, Mum. Why can't we look on it as a reward if I do well in exams? I'd work a whole lot harder. And you'd get your walking trip.'

She was still looking suspicious. Would she have to think there had to be more in it for me before she'd truly believe I wanted to go back? I thought of something. 'And I miss Dad,' I said. 'I'd get to spend a bit of time with him, even if he is busy.'

I could tell Mum was weakening, so played another good card. 'And if I ever decide to be an engineer, like Dad, it would look good on application forms. It would go down as work experience.'

The last two swung it from a 'no' to a 'we'll see'. And in spite of Toby's theory that 'we'll see', with

Mum, always ended up being, 'no', this time things worked out well. One of her walking friends phoned the next evening to try to persuade her to think again about coming along with the gang. She even told Mum I was plenty old enough to stay home by myself.

Home by myself? Dream on! That sorted it. Mum got in touch with Dad that very night to fix it up. He told her that the road to the Endlands was mostly open again, and if she could find a way to get me as far as Topane, he'd borrow some sort of vehicle and come to pick me up. After the call (which I'd been listening to in any case) she told me, 'Your dad sounds really keen. I warned him, though. I said, "If you end up involving Louie in one more natural disaster, I'll come out there myself and *murder* you."'

'What did he say?'

She smiled. 'He said that being killed by me would be an absolute pleasure.'

'I *told* you,' I reminded her. 'I said he misses you and wants you back.'

I waited for, 'We'll see'. And I was pleased that fatal phrase of hers rang only in my head. Mum didn't say it – not out loud.

The last weeks of term went by quickly enough. I did revise hard for exams. (I quite like taking them. I like the way that you can guess some of the questions in advance, and work out what you'll write. I like being handed crisp new examination sheets to scrawl all over and never see again. I like the fact that each exam lasts exactly the length of time you've been told, and not a moment longer. No dragging things out, like in class, because someone's mucking about, or writing so slowly they haven't caught up yet. Put one foot out of place in these exams and you are frogmarched from the hall.)

The last one was biology. I handed my paper to Ms Fannon as she came down the line of desks. We weren't allowed to speak until we were out of the hall, so I'd only just begun to tell Will what I thought of it when he interrupted. 'Never mind that, Louie. All done and dusted. Tell me about the holidays. Is what my mum said true?'

'What did she say?'

'That your mum's changed her mind about their walking trip, and you're back off to Creepsville-on-Sea?'

For a moment he'd baffled me. 'Creepsville?'

'You know,' he said impatiently. 'The beach where that tsunami happened.'

'Oh. Causeway Bay.'

He grinned the way you do when you know better. 'It's got a couple of new names now. Everyone's calling it Weirdsville-on-Sands. Or Spookstown.'

I tried to keep my end up. 'Everyone who's never been there.'

'And everyone who never wants to go.' He dragged his school bag off the pile outside the hall. I dug for mine while he persisted. 'So, did you see it?'

'What?'

'The footage that went up last night. On *Uncanny Bay*. Arif sent it around.'

Arif's forever sending round quite boring things. But I can't be the only person in the world who dislikes other people knowing more than me about things that are more to do with me than them. So, 'Sure,' I told Will. 'I've seen *that*.' And I was glad when he rushed off. 'Sorry. Can't hang around. Gran's taking us out to celebrate the end of my exams.'

I searched for it that evening after Mum had gone to bed. I'm not supposed to be online that late at night, but this was special. Mum doesn't believe in anything supernatural. (And, if she did, she would keep quiet about it rather than have to listen to lectures from Dad.) Still, I didn't want her thinking that I was starting to take an interest in anything spooky. She would assume at once that it had something to do with Toby's death, and maybe even ask herself if I was trying to work out some way of getting in touch with him. Something like that. She would be horrified. And very, very worried.

I'd made sure my door was firmly closed, and in a small hollow under the bed covers lifted the lid of my laptop and followed Arif's link. First, some sort of professor talked about the people on the bay. She said that it was all too easy for City dwellers in the Central Belt to think of them as simply backward in their attitudes. Their culture, she informed us, was coloured by the melancholy isolation of the bay. (Up came some photos of the beach in strangely coiled sea mists.) They had a history of eerie tales, she said, and used to gather on the sands at certain phases of the moon to share them. There was a name for these stories. They were called 'Malouy', and people who told them were very much respected – even honoured – in the community.

Malouy, she said, was rather hard to explain, but it

was a sort of *gloom* that ran through their culture like letters stamped through a stick of seaside rock. (That's exactly how she described it.) She said it was one of the most important features of these peoples' lives. So, it was not surprising, this professor said, that after the tsunami, even more of these grim and miserable stories were flying about. Their whole culture had taken a beating. The water hadn't just carried off their children, parents and friends. It had also washed out their local graveyard and swept away their buried dead, along with their memorial stones. Even the tiny traditional shrines of flowers and candles that many still kept in a corner of the home were washed away, along with photographs of the more recent dead, and keepsakes and written memories of their ancestors.

These people were, she said, bereft now. Utterly bereft.

'And,' she said, 'it is in this context that we should interpret everything that's been uploaded on this site.'

If I am honest, I suspect I might have closed my laptop down then. I would have left seeing the rest till morning, till daylight, when Mum would be up, running the shower and banging cupboard doors, and making things seem normal. But weekday mornings were a rush. Best not to risk her catching me on my laptop so early.

And after that I'd be in school, with Will seeking me out at any moment to ask me what I thought of something on the site. If I'd not seen it, I would be found out.

I pressed the pulsing arrow at the bottom of the screen, and I moved on.

FIFTEEN

We knew that hauntings would follow

The next piece of footage to come up showed two men.
The taller one stood close to the other but half a step
back, as if he were some sort of bodyguard. There, but
not there. He stared ahead blandly, as if into nothing and
nowhere, but the man in front looked directly into the
lens of the camera. The moment he opened his mouth,
I turned the sound way down, in case it alerted Mum,
then up again enough to hear what he was saying. His
accent was strangely lilting, almost sing-song.

'The earthquake cracked things wide open,' he said.
'We knew at once that hauntings would follow.'

'What sort of hauntings?' came a disembodied voice
behind the camera.

'Like this,' he said, and swung his left arm gently,
not at all fast, round in a full sweep. It cut right through

the body of the man who stood close – cut straight through him, coming out the other side.

The camera shook for a moment, still picking up the image of those two calm men standing so close to one another, like good friends. And then the image broke into a swirl of background. The sky tipped over and the ground heaved up. The camera shuddered to rest, showing a strip of something grey and grainy, that looked as if it might be sand.

The footage came to an end.

The next thing I clicked on couldn't have been more different. First came a printed announcement:

Interview with Five Ladies from Topane

Topane. The little mining town the pumping station had been there to serve, and where Dad planned to pick me up. It was a short way inland, which would explain why, when the film began, the tracking shot along a line of drab houses on a narrow street showed them to be undamaged by the wave.

The camera settled on the door of one of the houses, then we were inside.

From silence, there was suddenly a rush of noise. Five women crowded in front of the camera, all talking at once in some strange language that I didn't understand. When they weren't simply speaking over one another, they were interrupting and correcting. '*Neh!*' I kept hearing. '*Neh!*' The atmosphere appeared to be electric, but after a moment or two, something the interviewer said managed to calm them down enough for him to start with his questions. The women's voices were faded down. I'm sure that anyone who understood the language would still, if they listened hard enough, be able to hear what they were saying. But now the voice of a female interpreter could be heard above theirs, speaking fast to keep up.

'So, she appeared in the doorway, looking exactly like herself.'

'In one of the skirts she often wore.'

'We were all terrified. We knew that she was dead. Her husband had seen her swept away.' The camera panned across their faces as one of the women repeated, 'Swept away! No doubt about it. Her husband saw it happen.'

'Then, three weeks later, there she was in the doorway! She just walked in.'

'Just as if nothing had happened. Nodding and smiling the way she always did.'

They all agreed on that. The camera watched them

nodding at one another. 'Yes! Yes! Exactly the same!'

The interviewer asked a question in the women's language. One of them answered, 'No, because none of us knew how to start. How do you speak to someone you know is dead? What do you say?'

'So, we just waited, and she sat down in her usual place.'

The interviewer must have asked the women what they meant by 'her usual place' because all of them turned to point, and the camera panned over to a padded chair under the window.

'She always took that chair. We sew while we chat, so we agree the person with the weakest eyes should have that seat by the window, in the best light.'

'Her eyes were never strong. Even as a child, she used to have trouble.'

The interviewer asked another question. This time, the women looked a good deal more uneasy than excited.

'No, we offered her nothing, neither to eat or drink. None of us dared.'

'Perhaps that was wrong of us. We've wondered if that's why she didn't stay – just got up suddenly, went to the door, walked out.'

'And vanished!'

'We rushed to look, but there was no one on the street. You've seen how far it is to both the ends. No gaps. No alleys. She had simply *vanished*.'

One of the women shook her head as if she was ashamed. 'We worry that we should have *told* her. We think perhaps we should have asked her to stand up. Then she'd have seen for herself.'

The interviewer made a questioning sound.

In answer, one of the women pointed again. 'She would have seen the chair. Seen that, by sitting down on it, she'd made the padding soaking wet.'

Then came the very last question. And the answer. 'Because it was *sea* water. You could smell it. There were even shreds of weed.'

'Here. This far inland! Sea water!'

'We should have *told* her she was already dead.'

SIXTEEN

There, but not there

I didn't want to look at any more. Closing the laptop, I slid it on to the floor and pulled the bed covers up over my head. It was a comfort to know that Toby wouldn't have felt nearly as rattled as I did. He took a disbelieving line on pretty well everything we saw on screens. A lot of that came from his being older, and always needing to know more, and better. But he'd always been fascinated in how people who made films created their illusions.

I knew a bit myself. Toby and Jimmy St George had smuggled me into quite a few horror films while I was underage. ('The minute we give you the nudge, look down, Louie. Pretend to be digging for something in your pocket till we're past her.') I knew as well as he did how things on film could look so real that it was hard not to believe your eyes.

When we were watching *King Zomb*, the sharpened knives and hatchets and spades were swung about to cut the walking dead to pieces over and over, and still they kept coming. So that first bit of footage would have been a doddle to fake.

And in the second, there was nothing to see except a gang of women crowded round, telling a story. They could all have been actors. People will go to huge amounts of effort to post weird things. 'Right,' I said, once I'd conjured up my brother beside me in the bed. 'What do you reckon?'

I knew he would have answered, 'It could be either.'

'Real or fake, you mean?'

'If you believed in stuff like that, it could be real, I suppose. But if you think the supernatural is rubbish, it has to be a fix.'

'So, you do think it's a fix?'

'It's creepy,' Toby admitted.

'Isn't it?'

We lay together for a while, and then he tempted me. 'One more? Shall we watch just one more, to check? See if we can decide.'

'It's very late.'

'Chicken!'

'Not chicken. It's just that I have to get up in the morning.'

Even as I was letting the excuse form in my head, I felt guilty. I have to be at school by twenty to nine, but Toby will never have to get up to go anywhere ever again. He's dead. He's a few scrunchy ashes scattered on a hillside we used to climb together. (Toby was always in front.) He has no life at all.

He could still wheedle, though. 'Oh, come on, Louie. Five minutes won't make any difference. Let's watch one more.' He put on a deep, dramatic film narrator's voice. 'Don't be afraid, little brother. Step with me into the Kingdom of Shadows.'

'Oh, all right!' I reached down to pick up the laptop and we went back to the site.

'This one,' said Toby.

We watched. A camera panned along the wide white sands of the bay. I only recognised the place because of the knuckles on the ridge behind. High up the beach, several low huts had been built – the sort of temporary buildings you see behind the lines of tents in long-term refugee camps. Then came a voice-over:

'This is the ill-fated Causeway Bay, six weeks after the tsunami. As you can see, volunteers have already successfully cleared it of much of the detritus from the disaster.'

The camera slid around to show a group of men and women in work gear – jeans, dungarees and boiler suits – cheerfully chatting as they made their way, mostly in pairs, across the beach towards two trestle tables. A stack of plates and heaps of cutlery lay on one table, and several enormous bowls and serving dishes sat on the other.

The voice picked up again. 'But is this unhappy bay now cleared of everything?'

The camera watched the workers reach a part of the beach where one of the streams of water that tumbled down the ridge had hollowed out a narrow channel to the sea. It didn't look at all deep. But you could tell that it would be a problem if you wanted to keep your trainers or your work boots dry, so somebody had laid a couple of planks across, side by side, to make a little bridge.

That's when the film turned strange, because the workers didn't cross. Not only did the two or three in front not put a foot on the planks, but they stepped back, and it was clear that they had fallen silent.

At first, it looked as if nothing at all was happening.

On one side of the makeshift bridge, the workers were hanging back. The other side was clear, and a little way up the beach, the food was waiting on the trestle table.

And then a shadow passed across the bridge. Only a shadow. The sort of tall and elongated shadow a body makes at sunrise and sunset. I can't claim that the figure was clear. The best way to describe it would be sort of 'there, but not there'.

Still, you could definitely see it.

Another shadow followed. Then another, and another.

And all the time that this was happening, the group of workers were just standing back with troubled faces, waiting. Nothing appeared to be said. Nobody seemed to turn to the person beside them and pass a comment. They just all stood there, almost as if entranced.

One last tall, drooping shadow passed. There was a pause, and then two of the waiting workers stepped forward in turn to cross the empty bridge. In dribs and drabs others followed, and by the time that everyone had reached the tables, some were obviously talking again, but not with nervous excitement like the women in the film we'd seen before. They were just chatting idly, as if nothing the least bit odd had taken place.

121

Such a chill ran down my spine. 'Now that was seriously weird.'

As usual, Toby tried to be more knowing. 'It could be trick photography. Or they could all be actors.'

'Actors?'

I ran the footage back to just before it ended, with the workers at the trestle tables reaching for hunks of bread and spooning dollops of some chunky-looking green stuff on to their plates.

I found the face I'd spotted and touched the screen to make it bigger. 'These people aren't *all* actors, Toby. Take another look. That is our *dad*.'

SEVENTEEN

Things can get…'difficult'

I look back now, and wonder why seeing those bits of footage on *UncannyBay* hadn't put me right off the plan of going to see Dad. I could have made any excuse – saying I hoped to be invited on Will's family's camping trip, or even saying that I'd changed my mind and would be happy trailing along with Mum.

But days went by, and I said nothing, even when Mum admitted that she'd found a bus that, once a week, went from Sachard to Topane. The day she drove me to Sachard, she was more nervous than I was, endlessly spooning out safety advice.

'Yes, Mum… No, Mum… Of course, Mum… Yes, I'll remember that.' Jesus!

We found the bus. The way she fussed at the driver, you would have thought I was a toddler or an idiot.

'His dad should be coming to meet him. He's fairly tall, with brown hair. Thinning a bit on top, but—'

The driver interrupted. 'I expect that the lad will recognise his own father.'

Mum took the point. 'Well, anyhow, his dad's supposed to be there. And if he isn't, they're to meet in the Topane Hotel.'

My turn to worry. 'Why *wouldn't* Dad be there?'

Mum spread her hands. 'You tell me. But he did keep going on about the state of the roads.'

That did make sense. I'd not forgotten how bad they'd been even before the earthquake. But they were certainly a lot worse now. The bus took what was supposed to be the better road, the one that arched around to come into Topane from the north, yet still the journey seemed to last for ever. Time and again, some set of temporary work traffic lights would hold us up, sometimes for so long that even the driver, who'd been using that particular route for weeks, began to mutter that they must be stuck on red. There were diversions on to stony side tracks, and the road itself had several landslips that had not been cleared. It was impossible to drive at any speed and after a while the driver stopped apologising for the lengthening delay.

We could see all his energies were going into keeping his temper.

I slept a bit, then opened the book Ms Nyland had pressed on me as soon as Will told her I was off to the Endlands. 'You'll find this *fascinating*, Louie.' *Our Province Story*, it was called. But it was so boring, stuffed with great long paragraphs about negotiations and legislation and treaties, with almost nothing about the people there, and only a couple of pages on the two Coastal Wars, and the Endlanders' years of resistance. So, after ploughing through the first two chapters, and flicking through the rest, I just gave up and fell asleep again. When I woke, I was so hungry that I ate my sandwiches, then lost control and wolfed down not just the slabs of cake that Mum had packed for me, but also the ones that she'd put in for Dad. Moist gingerbread – his very favourite. I knew I'd have to confess, and fast, in case when Dad was next in touch with Mum, she asked him how he'd liked it. They weren't so separated yet that things like that wouldn't come out.

That set me thinking about how I'd go about asking Dad about the weird stuff I'd been watching on *UncannyBay*. We'd spoken regularly enough, but not about that. Was it because I didn't want him to think that being curious about the things I'd seen was the main reason I was going back? Or that I'd rather neither of my parents knew that I'd been logging on night after night to see what strange new things had been uploaded? I knew the reason I'd never mentioned it wasn't because I'd managed to persuade myself you can do anything with film, even make strangers part of your clever staging. If I had truly believed it was a fix, I would have told Dad straightaway so he could go on to the website himself and show the people he was working with the clever way in which they'd all been turned into some film buff's brainchild.

We got there hours late. Dad wasn't in the small town square. Most of the other passengers stumbled away, up a few unlit side streets. The driver had forgotten I existed, so I just followed two last passengers towards the shabby building with enough peeling letters above the door for me to know it was the Topane Hotel. I stood behind the pair who'd beaten me to the front desk, wondering whether I'd have to ask for a room, or if I could explain I was just waiting for my dad.

That's when I noticed he was there already, flat out on a padded bench along the lobby wall, and fast asleep.

He wasn't easy to wake, but finally he roused himself. 'Oh, God! I'm sorry, Louie! Closed my eyes for a moment, and...' Levering himself upright, he hugged me. 'How *are* you? It's been *weeks*. You're looking fit and well. What *time* is it?' He inspected his watch. 'Christ! Really?'

'The road was horrible.'

Dad picked up his jacket. 'Tell me about it! A pipeline to bring water to Topane some other way took full priority. Everything went into that, rather than road repairs.' He steered me towards the door. 'Still, that bus company should be more honest about how long the journey takes.' He led me to a battered car parked on the square. 'Awful for you, of course,' he added as he slung my bag on the back seat. 'But I should be grateful. First time for ages I've not been woken every half an hour by creaking bunk beds or bouts of hefty snoring.'

I made a face. 'Is it that bad in the huts?'

'No, no. I'm mostly joking.'

While we were driving out of Topane, he told me a little more. He started by apologising about the food. 'Of course, it depends who's cooking. But all too often it's only lukewarm, and rather tasteless. And almost all the volunteer cooks are vegetarian or vegan.

I sometimes think that, if I come across a stray sheep on the ridge…'

'Excellent plan, Dad! You and Valentina could become rustlers, and make a fortune.'

He didn't laugh. It was quite obvious that there was something else he wanted to get said. 'Louie, about you being here…'

'What?'

'It's a bit hard to explain. But there's a very definite atmosphere round here right now.'

It never occurred to me he meant it was a good one. He went on, 'That's hardly surprising. These are a proud and independent people who know they need our help but hate to have it. We've swooped into their home ground, and we can't help but make it obvious that we have a good deal more resources and more know-how.'

'You're telling me it's a bit "us and them"?'

He nodded. 'And they're *very* sensitive. So, we've developed a sort of policy to keep things cool. None of us go round taking photographs – not of the people or the place. It doesn't go down well. And most of us have learned, like I did, that's it's better to watch what we say, not just in front of them, but to the people back home.

Anything passed on ends up as public knowledge. They come to know about it, and they just don't like it. Things can get… well, let's just say "difficult".'

'So, don't go telling my schoolmates all about things here till both of us are safely home?'

'That's right. Not even Will. If you don't mind.'

I did feel cheated. I had been looking forward to sending Will vivid accounts of life in what we all now thought of as Uncanny Bay. But I could tell from the way Dad said, 'things can get difficult' that he meant 'nasty'. I didn't want him worrying about me, so I just said, 'He'd only think that I was bragging, anyway.'

'Right, then.' Relieved to have this tricky matter sorted, Dad turned the talk to me and my exams. 'Did the last couple of days go well?'

'I hope so.'

'Your mother says you settled down and worked really hard.'

'That was her deal for letting me come out here.'

He grinned. 'You have a very cunning mother.'

He asked some more about the days since we last spoke. Then, as we were both tired, conversation lapsed. Dad concentrated on driving, and, letting my head lean on the cool passenger window glass in spite of the endless jolting over potholes and bumps, I stared at the road ahead.

Moonlight is odd. I mean, you see it often enough. Everyone loves it. But no one ever just goes out to soak it up, the way they would if it were sunshine, or some brilliant ocean view. It's mostly wasted. Yet it's so beautiful. The silver sheen was picking out the shadows of the forest on either side. The night air had a blueish tinge, and everything – even the toiling engine of the car – seemed not just a whole lot quieter than in the day, but calm and magical. A different world. Maybe I was in that halfway to falling asleep and dreaming state. But when we drove around a sharpish bend hard up against the bottom of the ridge and I looked up to see half of a huge and anguished face carved on the rock above us, it seemed to me to be not just alive, but writhing in the half-light.

'Look!'

Dad screeched the car to a halt. 'What?'

'That face we saw before! Half of it's gone!'

Rolling his eyes, he speeded up again. 'You wouldn't get top marks in orienteering, Louie. The face we saw before was on the south side. This road comes in from the north.'

I didn't think I'd been that stupid. 'Well, it looks the same, except that half of it has fallen away.'

'There's a reason why they're identical. Apparently they both defend the same sacred place.'

'What sacred place?'

'I've no idea. Getting an answer to anything round here is harder than pulling teeth.' He waved ahead, towards a sprinkling of lights. 'See those? They're the emergency storage huts. Behind them is a sort of chalet where the Hendersons stay. He's the commissioner they sent, in charge of sorting out the stuff that comes by road. That's where we're spending the night. We'll take the car back to the bay in the morning.'

'It's pretty well morning now.'

'Not quite. And out here, every minute of sleep makes your life easier.'

'I realised that,' I said, 'as soon as I spotted you flat-out in the hotel.'

'Don't tell your mother,' he warned. 'Whatever you do while you're here, don't tell your mother that I wasn't there to meet you off the bus.'

EIGHTEEN

What boy?

'Whatever you do while you're here…'

I thought about that when I woke because, though I'd been counting the days to getting on the bus, I'd still been wondering what I'd be doing after I arrived. I knew I'd been registered for a bed in the bunkhouse as a volunteer. But I had no special skills. I was convinced that all the rest would have been chosen for their experience in things like refitting pipes, or building walls, whereas I had been given a place just as a favour to Dad, who'd only said, each time I asked about it, 'Don't worry about that, Louie. I'm sure you'll be able to make yourself useful.'

'Oh, well,' I told myself. 'It's not for all that long.' I lay there, staring at the Hendersons' chalet rafters for a while before looking around. Dad's bed was already empty, so, reckoning that he'd be keen to get the car back to whoever owned it, I forced myself to get up and take what I presumed might be the last good shower for a while.

I found Dad eating toast on a sort of rickety veranda that sloped alarmingly.

'Want some?' He pushed a tub of honey my way as I sat down. 'There's jam, too. But that's in the fridge.'

'So, the electricity's back up on this side?'

He jerked a thumb towards the ridge. 'Over there, too. And running water. In fact, a good number of the fishermen have habitable houses again. The clinic's sorted. The school room's looking good. Even the road along the bay is nearly finished.' He poured more coffee for himself. 'In short, we've done a brilliant job of clearing up. I reckon, if you didn't know…'

His voice trailed off, and he went back to munching toast.

I knew Mum's question would have been a very acid-sounding, 'So why are you still here?' Instead, I asked, 'What's still to be done?'

'Oh, just a few last things.' He stared into space as though he was mentally listing them, then snapped his attention back to tell me cheerfully, 'But I will definitely be coming home with you at the end of your stay.'

'Good!' I said. 'And Mum will be really pleased too.'

Dad pushed his coffee mug aside. 'Get on with your breakfast,' he told me. 'I have to go in the office over there to sort a few things out. You'll be all ready to go when I come back?'

'No problem. My bag's still packed.'

He wandered off towards the outbuildings and sheds behind us. I ate a slice of toast, and then another. That's when I saw the child stumbling towards me down the road. He was in shorts and a T-shirt that was far too big for him, and he was covered in mud. Right from the start, I thought that it was odd, a boy as young as that getting that muddy so early in the day. Was he in trouble?

I watched to see where he was going. I suppose I was thinking that he would stay on the road, and walk towards the few small shanty houses I had seen the night before, a little further along. But he turned off towards the veranda where I was sitting, and as he came closer I saw the path behind him was speckled with a gleaming brown.

The child was dripping water.

I scrambled to my feet. 'Are you all right? Did you fall into something?'

It was as if he hadn't really seen me. I mean, his pale eyes did meet mine, but only for a moment, then he went back to staring straight ahead. He had an air of determination, and seemed strangely calm. I was quite sure that, when I was that age, if I had fallen into water, or even been that badly soaked by a friend, I would have bawled my head off all the way home.

He reached the veranda, but then walked on past.

I hurried down the rickety veranda steps, sure there was something wrong. 'Hey! Hang on a bit!' I wondered if he only spoke the local language and didn't understand me. But by the time I'd followed him as far as the corner of the chalet, the child had vanished. The only person in sight was a tall man with ruffled, silvery hair striding towards me down the narrow passage between the chalet and the next outbuilding.

He smiled. 'Oh, hi. You must be Philip's boy, come to help out. I'm Broderick Henderson, the acting commissioner.'

Totally ignoring the hand that he'd stuck out, I stared past, down the passage. 'Where did the boy go?'

The tone turned sharp. 'What boy?'

'The one who just went past you.'

I *knew* I hadn't imagined it. All down the passage

were those splodgy wet patches on the ground. Footprints. But even as Broderick Henderson turned to glance behind him, I knew that no one, not even a running child, could possibly have vanished in the time that it had taken me to reach the corner.

Mr Henderson turned back. Running his hand through his silvery haystack of hair, I heard him mutter irritably, 'Oh, for God's sake! *Another* one?'

I thought at first he meant the wet boy who had disappeared. But then I realised he meant *me*.

NINETEEN

Knee-deep in ghosts

It isn't easy, being glared at like a troublemaker, and I was glad when Dad came round the corner and took Mr Henderson off. 'Broderick, I need to know how many of these cannisters I can take with me.'

So it was Mr Henderson's wife who explained. She suddenly stepped out of one of the other buildings, and caught me staring uneasily after my dad and the commissioner. 'You're Louie, aren't you? Was there a problem with my husband?'

I don't know what it was that made me open up and tell her everything. I suppose I still felt shaken. And it was obvious that Dad and Broderick Henderson were friends. I didn't want to let Dad down, so I told Mrs Henderson ('Julia, *please!*') about the strange boy that I'd seen, ending up rather pathetically, 'And what I told your husband seemed to upset him.'

She laughed. 'You mustn't take it personally.'

'He definitely wasn't pleased.'

'He wouldn't be.' She saw my anxious face, and tried to explain. 'All this 'uncanny' business is driving Broderick mad. The man was raised to think of it as stuff and nonsense. He doesn't believe in spirits. He thinks that when you're dead, you're dead, and there's an end to it. He reckons every haunting in the world is either someone's feverish imagination or some clever trick.' She waved a hand. 'And here he is, poor lamb, only twelve weeks from blissful retirement and puttering among his precious roses, and his superiors are mean enough to send him here. Now he's knee-deep.'

'Knee-deep?'

'In ghosts.'

She'd said it. Just come out with it. 'Ghosts.' And hearing this Julia say the word so calmly aloud, I could have *hugged* her. I was neither feverish nor mad. I'd just seen what I'd seen.

She was still cheerfully explaining. 'Poor Broderick. He keeps trying to persuade himself that everyone who sees these things has got themselves into some strange mental state because of the sheer awfulness of the tsunami – the horrible destruction and the deaths. And then...'

She stopped. It seemed to me that she was almost chuckling.

'And then?'

'Someone like you shows up, and before you're even over on the other side of the ridge you're seeing them too.' She was still smiling. 'The problem is that Broderick's a practical man, and to his way of thinking, none of this has any logic to it. He doesn't know what to do. If it was a brush fire, he could order in helicopters to drop water bombs. If it was plague, he could quarantine the victims. If it was famine, he could fly in food. But he can't deal with this because it's simply one wet ghost after another.'

That sounded really weird to me. 'Are they *all* wet?'

'Oh, yes. That's something you'll soon notice. They're all soaking wet. That's how they died, after all.'

The sheer relief that she believed me had begun to melt away. I was unnerved to realise that, not only did Julia naturally assume the boy I'd seen was a ghost, but she was confident that, having seen him, I'd see plenty more. The down-to-earth way in which she spoke of them was horribly unsettling. Ghosts. Spirits.

Spectres. Who would expect someone they'd only just met to talk about people who aren't really there as calmly as if they were casual passers-by, or neighbours from down the street?

I needed to check something. 'So, you've seen them, too?'

'Oh, yes.' She seemed completely unperturbed. 'There have been dozens round here.' She pointed down the road. 'All going that way. Not that I realised at first, of course.' She smiled. 'Well, you wouldn't, would you? There was no talk of ghosts before we came.' She started back towards the chalet and I fell in step with her. 'Broderick was sent out a few days after the disaster, and I thought I'd hitch a ride.' She gestured towards the ridge. 'I'm a geologist, and this is a deeply interesting area for rock formations.' She caught the look on my face. 'Oh, I know! That makes me sound as if I were just cashing in on a free trip after a tragedy. But I did hope to be helpful. And once I'd seen the horrible, horrible destruction…' Her voice trailed off, and when she spoke again she sounded more subdued. 'Well, let's just say that, since I arrived, I've sorted out ton after ton of emergency supplies, and I've not had a moment to lift my hammer to tap a single rock.'

Did that remind her time was passing? I watched her glance over the veranda rail that we were standing beside. Her eyes fell on the breakfast plate I'd abandoned.

'If you're done...?'

'I've finished, yes,' I said, adding politely, given that it had only been toast, 'it was delicious.'

'Your dad seems to have vanished. You'd better come and keep me company while I sort out more stuff he might be able to take with him.'

She didn't seem to ask herself if I'd prefer to stay where I was while I was waiting for him. Exactly as if she were one of my teachers in school, she simply set off for another of the outbuildings, expecting me to follow. She waved a hand at one of the large sheds as we passed. 'That's where I keep myself busy, sorting out supplies for the clinic. We didn't get much sleep at first. That stretch of road between here and Topane was so bad in those first few weeks that deliveries arrived at all hours.' She gave a little shudder. 'I'm still surprised we made it here ourselves. We practically destroyed our car while driving here from that fleabag hotel.'

She stopped, staring along the road in the direction Dad and I had come the night before. I thought she must be thinking about landslides and fallen trees and potholes. But, no, she was remembering something else. 'That's when I saw my first.'

'Your first?'

'Spirits. It was just getting dark. I'd finally unpacked the last of the stuff Broderick and I had brought with us in the car. You've seen how deep the shadows get round here at evening time. Well, I was idly staring up the road, and saw this family walking.' She wrapped her arms around herself as if she suddenly felt chilled. 'I can still picture them clearly. Two parents, with someone who looked as if he might have been a grandfather, and three small children. They were all covered in mud. Just dripping with it, all of them, from head to toe. The odd thing was that they were staring as if it wasn't *them* that looked so odd, but me. And I stared back. I wasn't frightened. Not at all. I was simply thinking, 'How did this family ever get so muddy and bedraggled? They must have done something really silly for the whole lot of them to get in such a mess.'

She pulled her cardigan more tightly round her shoulders. 'And then, just as I had begun to wonder if those poor children still had far to walk, and if I ought to offer them a lift, they all began to flicker.'

'Flicker?'

'Yes. In the half-light. Like when old films snag on the reel and start to judder.' She looked me in the eye. 'And then the family was gone. Poof! Vanished.'

'Like that wet boy who just went round the corner?'

She barely heard. 'One moment there. The next, a fading image.' She paused, then said, 'The thing is, Louie, there was something even more strange about them than the fact that they weren't really there.'

I waited.

'Not a single one of them was crying. Look what had happened. They'd all drowned, every last one. Suddenly and horribly. The entire family. But none of them, not even the smallest of the children, cried.'

TWENTY

Out of nowhere

That's when Mr Henderson and Dad strode back into view.

'Philip!' said Julia, taking his hand and shaking it warmly. 'Your lovely son and I have just been having the most interesting chat.'

Mr Henderson looked wary, as if he could only too easily guess what we might have been discussing. But Dad simply asked her, 'Oh, yes, Julia? About what?'

I saw her hesitate, but I'm not sure why I stepped in so quickly to say, 'Mrs Henderson told me she's a geologist.'

She gave me the warmest smile, and Broderick Henderson seemed relieved. 'Yes,' he chimed in. 'Julia says this is a *fascinating* area for rock formations. It's just a pity she's had so little time to look around.'

His wife brushed off the sympathy. 'Oh, I have seen a bit.'

Dad grinned. 'You'll certainly have seen that ghastly leering face.'

She couldn't resist correcting him. 'That's not a *rock formation*, Philip.' Then, maybe wondering if she'd been rude, she added kindly, 'But I certainly hope you didn't let Louie miss that.'

'No,' I said. 'I've seen both those faces now.'

I'd startled her. 'I didn't realise there were two.'

Was it Dad's tease about my orienteering skills that made me show I'd worked out where things were? 'We came past the broken one last night. The other's south of here, just past The Causeway.'

'That pumping station?'

'Yes,' Dad confirmed. 'Where Louie and I were when the earthquake struck and we had our lucky escape.'

'*Extremely* lucky,' said Broderick Henderson. 'I'm told the place is not much more than heaps of rubble now.' He shrugged. 'Still, maybe one day I should go and take a look.'

Even before Mum put me on the bus, I had been thinking I'd like to see the pumping station again.

Getting out had been such a scramble, and not one of us had thought to ask Miles to dust off his phone and take a few photos. I'd realised from what Dad had said that I wasn't going to be allowed to flash my camera about once I was on the bay. But here at least was a chance to show Will and my other mates at school real evidence of all the devastation I'd escaped. I didn't know how busy Dad would be once he got back to work, so I said to him, 'Can we go now? It wouldn't take too long. And we could even go a little further, to show Mrs Henderson the other scary face – the one that's still all there.'

Mr Henderson glanced at his watch, then at his wife, and you could almost see what he was thinking: *Why not? Get Julia back into her passion for rocks. Anything's better than all this stuff about spirits!* But she had turned to look at one of the sheds in which, presumably, the endless deliveries of supplies still needed sorting.

And then the weirdest thing happened. I suddenly heard Toby in my head. Clear as a bell, he was saying, 'She needs a map! Louie, quick! Show her a map!'

The shock I felt! Up until then, I had known perfectly well that it was always me who brought my brother to mind. Or, when he came, it was because something around raised echoes, either of his being

149

there, or of my wishing for it. But not this time. I'd not been thinking of Toby at all. I hadn't been missing him, and nothing around me was either a memory or a reminder.

His voice came out of *nowhere*.

He had a purpose though, I could tell. And it must have been a strong one, because that habit I'd always had of falling in with my big brother's orders led me to say the words out loud for him. 'We need a map.'

'Nonsense,' said Dad. 'It's just a short way down the road.'

But Mr Henderson was already halfway back to the chalet. 'We have maps. Louie's right. It might be sensible to take a look.'

As we caught up, he came back down the steps with two. 'That's just the roads and tracks. This is an aerial view.'

He spread them out on the veranda table. Mr Henderson and Dad studied the road map. I suppose they were checking for side tracks in case of any obstacles we came across, like fallen trees or sink holes.

Julia leaned over the aerial map. I stood beside her, but my thoughts were miles away. I was still taken up with Toby butting into my head like that, out of the blue. Not only had the sound of his voice interrupting that way shaken me badly, but somehow it was unwelcome, as if I'd suddenly lost control.

I heard Julia mutter, 'Now that is curious. You'd almost think that it had been designed.'

I looked to where she pointed and tried to pay attention. 'Sorry?'

'Here, look. See how this contour line repeats itself perfectly this way, but in reverse.' Her finger ran along one line on the map, then backtracked down another, tracing the long, narrow shape of a crocodile's mouth. 'See? The ridge side, and the forest side facing it, are perfect replicas.' She tipped her head. 'Like one of those illusions.'

'Illusions?'

'You know. You look at a silhouette and see a vase with two handles. Squint at it differently, and it becomes a face with sticky-out ears.' She stabbed the map with her finger. 'Same here.'

This time I watched more carefully as her finger moved. 'These lines mirror one another exactly. It's solid rock, so has to be coincidence. But it is curious.' She swivelled the map round so I was looking at it from the side. 'Especially since it makes another of those faces.'

I saw it instantly – the face depicted by the contour lines. And not just any face, but long and cadaverous, exactly like the ones carved in the rock. That is the moment I heard Toby's voice again, loud and triumphant, '*Bingo!* Now she's on board. Oh, well done, bro! Well done!'

That was the first time ever, in my whole life, that I remember wishing that my brother was gone.

TWENTY-ONE

What is all this to you?

Why did I feel such unease? 'Well, done, bro!' was my brother's highest form of praise. I would have *longed* for him to say it any other time. But not right then. I had been busy looking at the map, and once again he'd broken in out of nowhere, nothing to do with me, and I felt what I had before – a horrible loss of control.

But what Toby said was right. Showing Julia the map had made all the difference. Now she was more than keen to see the narrow inland canyon. Even her husband was curious. 'You say that this undamaged face is just a short way past the Causeway Pumping Station?'

'Hardly any distance at all,' said Dad, laying a finger on the map to show him. 'We'd barely got over the shock of seeing it when we arrived.'

Broderick Henderson put his own finger on the map. 'And the other face is round about here?'

Dad nodded. 'That's right.'

I felt a nudge and turned to see Julia pointing to the same two places on our own map. 'See? Dead opposite again.' She asked my dad, 'Aren't they supposed to be guarding something? That's what I heard.'

'Some sacred place,' said Dad, and added ruefully, 'Can't be the pumping station. Or, if it was, they made a pretty poor job of it!'

Mr Henderson didn't get the joke. 'Philip, those faces must pre-date your pumping station by *centuries*.' He made up his mind and slid an arm round his wife's shoulders. 'What do you say, Julia? We wouldn't be gone long. Surely we've earned a couple of hours off.'

So, it was settled.

We went in their car, which was a good deal better than the one that Dad had borrowed. While Julia picked her way around the various hazards on the road, her husband studied the map. Dad and I sat in the back. He chatted with the Hendersons while I stared out of the window, barely listening, trying to work out how this little side trip had come about so fast. I knew that it was Toby who had swung the matter, and I think I was expecting him to sort of 'show up' again. I know I had the oddest feeling that he ought to do that, if only to apologise for overstepping the mark and coming over as a lot more real than he should seem, now he was dead and gone.

I suppose what I really wanted was to feel comfortable about his voice in my head again.

But there was no Toby, only the jolting getting worse and worse as we drove on. The steep ridge wall on one side was closing in steadily towards the trees on the other. Suddenly, Julia broke off what she was saying to Dad about sedimentary rocks. I looked ahead. A scraggy dog was limping down the road in front of us. It was horrifically thin, and picked its way along by raising each paw delicately in turn. 'Poor creature,' Julia murmured. 'Pads worn raw.'

I leaned between the two front seats. 'Couldn't we pick it up, and try to find its owner?'

Mr Henderson let out the most exasperated sound. It wasn't a clear 'No!' but it was just as irritable. I thought at first that was because he thought the dog would be a nuisance in the car, or give us fleas, or something. But Julia turned her eyes from the road just long enough to give me the sort of teacherly look that said, 'Oh, come now, Louie. Use your brains.' And that's when I realised that we'd passed no streams or rivers, but the dog was dripping wet.

Neither my dad nor Mr Henderson had even seen it.

Now Mr Henderson said nothing, simply lowered his head, pretending to study the map. Dad turned to me and raised an eyebrow. Did he assume he'd missed whatever I'd seen? Did he have any idea that some of us could see things that weren't exactly there? Of course, he'd missed my dripping boy, and Julia's talk of the wet family trudging down the road. And I'd not talked to him about the things I'd seen on *UncannyBay.* The look on Dad's face was just the baffled one I'd seen a hundred times at home, usually meaning, 'What's got your mother into such a mood?', or, 'Was I supposed to *know* that we were going out tonight?' Julia had said her husband was infuriated by the idea of spirits all around him.

But was it possible my father hadn't even *noticed* some of us were seeing them?

We drove in silence till Dad tapped my knee and jerked a thumb towards the side of the road.

'Remember? That's where the four of us climbed over to the bay.'

Julia slowed the car to even more of a crawl. 'Want to get out and take a look about?'

'No, let's press on to The Causeway.'

Broderick Henderson raised his head from the map. 'That's not what they call your pumping station on this.'

'I didn't think that map showed place names,' Julia said.

'Just a few ancient ones. Caves and stone circles. Sacred sites.'

'So which is this?'

'I've no idea. It simply calls the place *Spi Ruaradh*.'

Spi Ruaradh. The name sounded oddly familiar. Then I remembered. Those were the strange words written in faded pencil beneath one of the photos we had seen the night before the earthquake – that line of workmen looking so uneasy in front of what they'd built. The pumping station in its stages of construction. And then that final photo – really the first – of how the place had looked before work even began, showing that curious black fissure in the rock.

Spi Ruaradh – set dead between the scary faces. So if that truly was the place the rock carvings were there to defend, small wonder that those men had looked so guilty, and tried to hide their tools. Had they been bullied into doing the job? Bribed by good wages? Or had they simply got so used to dismal treatment they hadn't managed to summon up the will to refuse?

Had those first engineers trespassed upon a sacred site?

'Why did your firm build there, exactly?' I asked my dad.

'It wasn't our firm way back then,' he said. But obviously my question set him thinking, for as we neared the pumping station he was twisting in his seat to study the narrow strip of land under the ridge. 'Well,' he began. 'Most probably because…'

I'm sure Julia Henderson followed what he said. I know I didn't. To me, it was a claggy mass of words I didn't fully understand, like surface topography, and soil percolation, and overhang proximity. After a while, I sensed that Broderick Henderson had given up as well, and was relieved when his wife broke in by asking Dad, 'So, shall we stop?'

'No,' Dad said. 'Let's see the face first, and stop here on the way back.'

Nobody argued. We drove straight past the

pumping station ruins, and it seemed no time at all before Broderick Henderson, stabbing a finger on the map, and Dad, pointing ahead, both called out, 'Here!'

All of us scrambled out. Julia stared up at the long, looming face with its staring eyes and twisted mouth, and let out a gasp. 'My God! Now that *is* creepy!'

I knew what to expect, and this time I was seeing it in daylight. But still I felt the same old chill run down my spine.

Broderick Henderson took his wife's arm. 'Good lord! The anguish on that face!' He stared some more. 'What *skill* it must have taken, given the tools they had back then.' He shook his head. 'Dangerous work, too. That is some overhang.'

'They may have thrown up some sort of scaffolding,' suggested Dad.

We stood in silence after that. The thin white face stared down. I backed away a bit, then moved to the side. The eyes seemed to follow me. I moved away further, wondering how far the eyes could look as if they kept on watching me, only to find myself stumbling against one of the boulders scattered around. 'Ouch!'

Julia glanced my way. 'If those fell in the earthquake, then the face was lucky.'

That's when I heard Toby again, impatient and contemptuous. 'Not lucky, lady! Powerful!' It was so loud and clear I was convinced that all of them had heard, and would assume that it was me who spoke. But no one so much as turned to glance at me. Even Julia was back to staring at the face.

'What are you *doing*?' I said to Toby fiercely in my mind. 'Why are you even *here*? What is all this to you?'

But he was gone.

As we piled back in the car, Dad touched me on the arm. 'You look a little shaky. Did you get any sleep?'

'I'm fine,' I told him. 'Honestly.'

He laughed. Leaning towards the Hendersons in the front seat, he said, 'That tell-tale word. "Honestly". Sure sign a boy is hiding something!' He didn't press me though, and, leaning back, he quietly changed the subject. 'So, tell me, Louie. How will you feel about stopping at the station?'

'I'm curious to see the place properly again,' I admitted. 'And we should definitely take photos.'

'To freak out your poor mum?'

After his recent warning in the car, I didn't want to say it was to show my mates at school. I thought of something else. 'And to complete the set.'

'What set?'

It did surprise me that he had forgotten. 'That series that they had along the corridor. They'll still be in the rubble. They might be found when they rebuild.'

'Rebuild?' Dad's voice got louder, to include the Hendersons. 'No chance! Topane gets water from the north now. That temporary pipeline from Sachard will be made permanent.'

The car pulled up beside the ruined fence. Julia asked, 'So what will happen to this place?'

Dad burst out laughing, and pointed. 'Oh, come on, Julia! It's already happened! Look at that shocking mess.'

TWENTY-TWO

The place is so horribly crowded

Dad was dead right. If possible, the site looked even more of a disaster than before. I couldn't see that anything in particular had changed since that extraordinary morning, but somehow the heaps of rubble looked more abandoned now. More hopeless. The twisted scraps of metal scattered all about were already rusting, and sad, untidy clumps of weeds were growing all around.

Julia set off after my dad, picking her way with care over torn lengths of fence. I followed them into the compound, and thought at first the strangeness that I felt was something wrong with me. Dad had said I looked shaky, but suddenly I was all hot and bothered, and my skin turned clammy. Even my eyes weren't working properly. All around me were fleeting changes in the light, so fast that they were gone almost before I noticed, as if a host of birds were flying overhead, each of them blocking the sunlight for a flickering moment. But there were no birds up there. On every side, odd, shifting shadows kept on catching my attention, only to vanish.

But nothing was moving.

I wondered if I was reliving some of the shock the four of us had felt during the earthquake. But this was different. It was more... *baleful*, somehow, as if the awful thing that happened had left its mark on everything around – the chunks of fractured steel, the splintered door frames and the shattered roof. It was the way Ms Nyland told us she had sometimes felt on ancient battlefields – as if some echo of a terrible past still lingered in the air.

But we'd been really *lucky*, here in the compound. No one had died. And though the pumping station itself had been destroyed, buildings fall down or are demolished all the time. Why this cold, creepy feeling?

I wondered if I was the only one to notice the sheer strangeness of the place, so looked at the others. But they were all staring at their feet, so I looked down as well, to see a line of damp rising around my trainers. The stain of it was creeping steadily up and, as I watched, my feet turned cold and I felt moisture seeping through on to my socks.

Mr Henderson stepped up on a large and flattish stone. 'Talk about rising damp! Is it the water the station used to pump up to Topane that's turning this place into a swamp?'

Dad didn't answer. I could tell that he was puzzled. He had that look he gets when there's a problem to be solved. And even I could see that there was something very odd indeed about the compound because, although my feet were soaking wet now, great patches of the ground around seemed to be perfectly dry.

Mr Henderson turned to his wife. 'You're the geologist, Julia. Underground streams are up your street. What on earth's happening here?'

She, too, had stepped up on a boulder to save her shoes from getting any wetter. It was clear from her face that she was as baffled as my dad. Almost as if to fob her husband off while she was thinking, she muttered, 'Hidden water courses can be a bit of a mystery...'

'Until you find them,' Broderick Henderson responded cheerfully. 'And after that, of course, I expect they're mostly a nuisance.'

I don't believe she heard a word he said. Her anxious

look was deepening to something more like fear. And I knew why, because the creepy feelings I had were getting worse and worse. I tried to brush them off and pull myself together enough to look around some more – take a few photos of what was left of the place to show my classmates and Mum. But it was hopeless. As I came closer to the rubble piled against the ridge, the eerie feeling of unease got stronger and stronger, till I could hardly breathe.

'Just get a photo of the ruined building,' I told myself. 'Just get it done.'

I raised my phone. But at the moment when the camera was focusing, I felt myself swivelled sideways. *Click!*

Dad? Julia? Mr Henderson? I spun round, but there was nobody behind me – no one anywhere near. I looked at the screen, expecting to see a patch of sky or forest, or a segment of ridge. But it was misty pale all over, nothing there at all, and somehow shivering as if it weren't the still shot I had taken, but a living film.

I didn't stop to try to take the photo again. I took off, terrified. Clambering over the debris of a fallen wall, I hopped and jumped as quickly as I could over the rubble strewn across the compound, and back to the car.

Julia was already there, ashen-faced, in the driving seat. Seeing me careering towards her, she leaned across to open the passenger door so I could scramble in. 'There you go,' she said, as I threw myself on to the seat beside her and slammed the door shut. 'Safer in here by far.'

'Safer?' It seemed the oddest word to pick. Had she, like me, sensed something deeply disturbing? 'Do you think there's about to be another earthquake?'

'Oh, no,' she said. 'Nothing like that. It's just I couldn't stand being out there any longer. I could hardly breathe. The place is so horribly, horribly *crowded*.'

Then, realising what she'd just said, she, too, began to shake.

TWENTY-THREE

You think we've all gone bats?

The moment Dad and I were alone, I let rip. We'd said goodbye to the Hendersons, and were on our way back to the bay. I'd barely settled in my seat before I challenged him. 'Dad, you can't keep pretending everything round here is normal any longer. I have to know what you think is going on.'

He made a feeble stab at fobbing me off. 'Who says there's anything going on?'

'I do.' I started on my list. 'Miles rushing home. Whole websites about the soaking wet undead who haunt their friends. Weird places that give everyone the creeps. Ghost families traipsing down roads, leaving dripping tracks. Hidden springs rising up, but only in the patches around people's feet…'

I stopped. If I'd gone on, I would have mentioned

Toby's uninvited voice. I didn't want to do that. I simply waited for a moment, then prompted. 'Well?'

Dad made one last, stupid attempt to stall. 'Louie, can we please leave this till we get to the bay?'

But I'd had *enough*. And I was really scared by what had happened. 'No! No, we can't! You've been avoiding talking about this right from the start – for *weeks*. And I know the minute we reach the bay, you'll find someone who needs your help with this, or wants advice on that, and you'll make sure you're far too busy to talk.' I told him firmly, 'I'm not having that. I came down here to spend some time with you. I really want to do that. But if you're not prepared to tell me honestly what's going on, I'd rather go back home.'

That seemed to shake him. 'Home?'

'Why not? At least things are *normal* there. And Mum is straight with me. You're treating me like a fool.'

There was a silence while my dad drove on. At first, I thought I'd blown it totally – that we would reach the junction and, instead of doubling back along the brand new coast road, he'd drive on to Topane and leave me there to catch that awful bus back to Sachard. But I was wrong, because the very next time he spotted an unbroken strip of land beside the road, almost a lay-by, he swung the car to the side and switched off the engine.

'You're right, I haven't been straight,' he told me, staring blankly ahead. 'But, to be fair, I've not known where to start. How can I? I don't believe what's going on around me. I *can't* believe it. I don't believe in other worlds. I don't believe in wraiths or ghouls or ghosts or spectres, not any of that stuff.' His voice turned fierce. 'I think it's rubbish. Utter rubbish. What I believe – what I, a sensible man, know for a *fact* is when you're dead, you're dead. That's that. And anything else has to be something boiling away inside the mind of the person who believes they're seeing it.' He turned to look at me for the first time since he began. 'So how can I explain this stuff to you? I *can't*. I don't believe it! It can't be there! And my whole view of things – everything I know about the world, and everything I stand for – would simply collapse if I even *began* to credit all the weird things that seem to be going on around us now.'

I felt quite sorry for him suddenly, and didn't know what to say. In the end, I turned it into a question. 'You think we've all gone bats?'

He banged his palms down on the steering wheel so hard they must have stung. 'I don't know. I don't *know*! I have to think it's something to do with all the grief and loss.' He sounded pleading, almost desperate. 'It can't be anything else! This is a rational world, Louie! A rational world! It goes by rational rules. And these things are... are...'

He couldn't finish. He sat there, staring through the windscreen, probably seeing nothing, shaking his head.

So, what was I to say? What was I even to think? I couldn't criticise him any more for steering clear of saying anything about the strange things going on around him. If everything he'd ever seen, or worked on, had fitted in with how an engineer is taught to see the world – through all those laws of mechanics and gravity and thermodynamics and stuff – how could he ever come to terms with wraiths and spectres and things like that showing up out of the blue?

He couldn't. I could understand that.

I thought back to the very first bits of film I'd watched on *UncannyBay*. 'All right,' I said. 'So what about when you and the other workers stepped back to let those strange shades cross that thin plank bridge in front of you? What did you think that you were seeing then?'

He'd obviously seen the film himself because he

knew what I was talking about. 'Nothing that was exactly *there*.'

'But it was there enough to make you all stand back and wait your turn.'

Again, he shook his head. 'I simply can't explain that.'

'You can't dismiss it, either.'

Dad switched on the engine. 'Louie, it's getting late. I promised that I'd have this car back hours ago. You'll have to make your mind up very fast. Do I go on to drop you in Topane? Or are you coming to the bay with me?'

It wasn't hard to choose. He'd made as good a job as he could of trying to explain how difficult he found things. How could an engineer like him come to terms easily with things that broke the physical rules he'd gone by all his working life? Why, even Miles had run away from me, rather than talk about it.

'I'm coming to the bay with you.'

TWENTY-FOUR

Just listening?

The rules he'd gone by all his working life came up again only an hour later. We'd reached the bay. I'd dumped my backpack in the bunkhouse I was going to share with Dad and four other volunteers, and we'd only walked a short way along the beach before we ran into Valentina, standing on the wide sands and staring out at the waves.

We came up behind and Dad touched her on the shoulder. 'Look who's arrived.'

She spun round. 'Louie! You made it!' She gave me a giant hug. 'Things must look very different from when you were here last.'

I wasn't going to argue with that. 'Yes, very different.'

'We're getting there.' She waved a hand. 'You'll

know the new road's more than passable and most of the utilities are back in some form or another. And quite a few of the fishermen's houses are halfway to finished. It won't be long now.'

'I'm looking forward to helping.'

'Helping?' She shot my dad a look, and said, 'Phil, I thought he was just here to be with you for part of his summer break.'

'That too,' I said. 'But I can do stuff with you while I'm here.'

Now Valentina was looking even more suspicious. 'What sort of stuff?'

I couldn't work out what was bothering her. 'Anything. Whatever you're doing. I can just tag along and make myself useful.'

I knew at once I'd said exactly the wrong thing. Almost before I'd finished, she had turned to Dad. 'Phil, what are you thinking? Louie's had absolutely no experience. He's underage, so he can't be insured, either for accidents that he might cause, or any he has himself.'

Dad looked a bit embarrassed. 'Oh, come on, Valentina. He's a sensible lad. No reason he can't lend a hand.'

She wasn't having it. 'Come off it, Phil. You know as

well as I do that most of these volunteers don't bother with the most basic safety rules. They may be keen, but half of them don't have the first clue what they're doing, and are too proud to stop and ask. Working here isn't *safe*.'

'You two are doing it,' I pointed out.

'Yes,' she said sharply. 'Your dad and I *are* doing it. But we have years of experience on busy sites. We can see trouble coming.' She started in again on Dad. 'You can't even put him in the kitchen. That place is one calamity after another. Look at that lad flown out with those bad burns.'

I did at least think Dad would argue with her. But no. He stood there, all hangdog, like someone at my school getting an earful from a teacher. She turned back to me. 'I'm sorry if you're disappointed, Louie. But I'm afraid you'll have to treat this visit as a holiday. It's just a shame that you can't swim.'

Now I was really nettled. 'I *can* swim.'

She rolled her eyes at my stupidity. 'Not here, you can't. There's still all sorts of nasty stuff in the water. It's not safe.'

I pointed. 'So what are those fishermen doing out there on those boats?'

'Taking too big a risk, if they eat anything they catch,' she said.

When Dad still stood there without arguing, I realised this was a battle I wasn't going to win. Irritably, I asked Valentina, 'So what am I supposed to do all day, while Dad is working?'

'We'll think of something, Louie,' Dad said soothingly. He looked at Valentina hopefully. 'Could we perhaps lend him to Hugo? Hugo is looking for people.'

'Who's—?' I tried to ask, but Valentina was already swatting that idea away. 'For heaven's sake, Phil! The boy can't work for Hugo. He's *far* too young for that. And when you think—'

She stopped short.

'When you think *what*?' I demanded.

Dad obviously knew exactly what it was she was refusing to say. But he wouldn't spit it out, either. He just slid an arm round my shoulders. 'Honestly, Louie. We'll find you something to do. You won't be bored all day. Meanwhile, it will be lovely having you around. I'm glad you came.'

There didn't seem a way to start up the argument again, so we all left it there.

Two mornings later, I bumped into Hugo. He was, I

reckoned, younger than my dad and Valentina, but quite a bit older than Miles. He was quite short, with dark blonde hair that looked, even to me, as if it could have done with a wash. (My mother would have had him in the shower instantly.) He must have spotted me on the beach, waiting for Dad to come back from helping with some generator that had been acting up. He probably took me for an idiot, the way I was kicking up fringes of sand and jumping to and fro across the runnel of water that ran from a gully at the base of the ridge down to the sea. Still, even though he was limping badly, he did make the effort to come up to me and put out his hand to shake mine. 'It's Louie, isn't it? Phil's boy?'

Did everyone round here know *everything*? 'That's right.'

'You're waiting for your dad?'

I didn't want to sound even more lame than I felt. 'He'll be back any minute. I was just going to meet him.'

'I'm Hugo.' He fell in step with me along the sand. 'Your father told me you were here when it all happened. That must have been a fearsome sight.'

'Not here, exactly,' I corrected him. 'We were at the pumping station.'

'On the other side?'

I nodded. 'It must have been at least an hour afterwards before we reached the top there,' I pointed to the gap, 'and got to look down.'

'Still,' he said, 'you will have seen the place at its very worst.'

He sounded, curiously, as if that was a good thing.

'Yes, I suppose I did.'

'Extremely helpful.'

'Sorry?'

'Well, I was just thinking...' He started over again. 'I mean, I've been watching you hanging about here on the sands most of yesterday and all of this morning. You look a little bored.'

'I am bored,' I admitted. 'Each time Dad joins me, somebody rushes up to take him away again.'

He smiled. 'And all of them are no doubt saying, "Just for a minute, Phil. This won't take long," then keeping him for hours. Exactly what I thought.' He stopped in his tracks and pointed along the beach to two small cabins Dad had said were where he worked. 'So, I suppose I couldn't help wondering if you would like to make yourself useful.'

I didn't like to say that any idea of my helping

him had been swatted away by Valentina on the day I arrived. In any case, I was curious. And as I waited for Hugo to explain, he set off once again along the beach in his lolloping stride, like someone who'd been on a horse for several hours and hadn't quite got used to walking on firm land again. The cabins he was aiming for were getting closer, and thinking I'd prefer not to be taken by surprise by anything I found inside, I asked him, 'What did you have in mind?'

He answered, 'It's a little hard to explain. It's mostly just listening to what the locals want to say.'

That didn't sound madly helpful to anyone. 'Seriously? Just *listening*?'

Again, he smiled. 'That's about it. If we were anywhere but here, you'd also be having to pass out tissues, and dishing out what comfort you can. But Endlanders are different. Weeping's not something they do in front of strangers. So, yes, I think that I can safely say you'd mostly just be listening.'

I was still really confused. 'But if these people are too private to cry in front of somebody they don't know, why would they want to *talk* to them? Especially,' I added, 'to someone my age.'

We'd reached the cabin. Instead of going up the

two small steps and pushing open the door, he turned to look at me. There was a long, long pause, and then he said, 'Your father hasn't told you *anything*, has he? I mean, did Philip even mention Malouy?'

'Malouy?' The word sounded faintly familiar, and I remembered the professor on *UncannyBay*. 'Aren't they the eerie tales the locals like to tell?'

'Not so much eerie as *tragic*,' Hugo explained. 'And not so much "like to tell" as "are obliged to share".'

'I don't understand.'

Taking my arm, Hugo led me just far enough away that we would not be overheard by anyone who might be in the cabin. 'It's like this, Louie. Embedded in this culture is the belief that, if someone dies in an untimely or a violent way, or their body's disturbed after death, their spirit must be placated, or…'

He stopped, presumably to find the best way of describing it. But in the end, all he came out with was, 'Or it will sort of turn bad.'

Now I remembered what my dad had said. 'Spirits of Spite?'

He winced. 'That's maybe over-egging it.' Again I watched him search for words to explain. 'More that they become restless and troublesome – even a bit resentful, as if the members of the family who are still living have somehow let them down. That's where the listening comes in. Traditionally, the way to soothe an angry spirit is for the loved ones who are left to tell the story over and over.'

'The story?'

'Of the death. The early, violent or simply unexpected death.'

I turned my face away, towards the water. So that was why, when Valentina instantly dismissed this as a job for me, Dad had caved in at once. Early or violent or unexpected death? Toby's had been all three. So now I had to tell Hugo there was no way I'd be allowed to help him. He might as well save his breath.

Maybe he thought that I'd just turned to watch the lapping waves. In any case, Hugo kept talking. 'The story has to be gone through, over and over, in front of one witness or more. That is the only way to calm the spirit down, and it's the original meaning of Malouy.'

So, Dad had almost got it right. I thought back to the evening when that strange figure materialised behind him on the screen, listening to what he said before the picture and the sound cut out. Right at that moment,

Dad had been telling me about the Spirits of Spite, and what must be done to placate them.

'So it's a sort of *exorcism*?'

Reluctantly, Hugo nodded. 'I *so* dislike that term, and do try not to use it. But to be honest, that's about it – except, of course, that it's a whole lot gentler way of ridding the living of spirits than anything that horrible word brings to mind. Malouy's just the act of *telling*, you see. But part of that, and just as important, is the listening.'

I couldn't see the point of wasting Hugo's time. 'My dad won't want me listening to stories like that. You see—'

He interrupted me. 'I know. Your brother. I'm aware of that. But you won't actually know what anyone is saying. They all prefer to do Malouy in their own language. I will admit I learned a bit myself when I was studying anthropology, but I can handle it. I'm a trained counsellor.'

'Really? You mean, you understand their stories? But I'd just be sitting there with all this stuff they're saying rolling over my head? And it still *works*?'

Even to me, what I said sounded dismissive, and Hugo didn't look too pleased. 'Listen,' he said. 'Beliefs and practices like this don't spring out of nothing and nowhere. They're born of the experiences of generations and embody basic instincts. They stem from shared feelings, and the customs around them arise so the community can pass on lessons learned over the centuries.'

His tone was calm and polite. But it was still like being lectured by a teacher. Trying to sound a bit more positive, I said, 'I think if Dad knew that I wouldn't understand what they were saying, he might change his mind. And he and Valentina haven't found anything else that I can do round here. So I could ask him.'

I'm sure I hadn't sounded all that keen. Still, turning back towards the nearer of the two cabins, Hugo said, 'Why don't I show you where we are?'

Outside, the cabin was plain, with dull metal sides and a small frosted window. Inside, at the far end, were two large cabinets behind a desk littered with files and papers. Near the door was an old, stained sofa with stuffing leaking out. Someone had thrown a bright patchwork blanket over the back of it, so though it was the sort of thing you might see in a skip, it still looked cosy and inviting.

Beneath the window was a narrow shelf. I saw a

kettle on a lead, a set of mugs and tins of what I guessed were tea and coffee and sugar.

'You've got electricity?'

'Oh, yes. We're well-appointed.'

There was a silence while I pretended to look around again. I had the feeling Hugo wasn't going to tell me anything more unless I asked a question. Maybe, because of what I'd said, he'd changed his mind about my working with him. The thought annoyed me. I didn't want the job. It wasn't at all the sort of thing I'd hoped I'd be doing. But if Hugo was getting ready to tell me I wasn't right for it, I wasn't going to make it easy.

'Right, then,' I said. 'If Dad decides he's happy so long as they all talk in their own language, how soon can I begin?'

TWENTY-FIVE

One sad soul after another

The job was horrible. Horrible. (I didn't dare tell Dad.) I had to sit there quietly while one sad soul after another reeled out the story of how their child, or husband, grandmother or whoever, had died. In telling me I wouldn't understand a single word, and that these people weren't the weeping sort, Hugo had made a big mistake. They might have started off in their own language, but when they saw I wasn't following, as often as not they'd switch to mine. Perhaps they were being polite, but often I thought it was more likely that they needed me to show at least some real response. How can you talk about the moment your tiny son slipped from your grasp into a crashing black wave, and see no change at all on someone's face? No wince. No look of shock. Not even a flicker of sympathy. Absolutely nothing.

You *can't*.

The first one who came was so spindly thin that all the pale hair splayed around her face looked almost as if it might weigh as much as she did.

She'd started off at once. 'I lost my daughter, Elida. She was holding my hand. She had been acting up the whole way down the beach, but I couldn't turn and take her home because I had agreed to meet her grandmother to pick up a mended net. Elida fussed and whined. She kept on dragging her feet, and when I tried to pull her along faster, she forced her toes deep in the sand.' The woman's bony fingers fiddled with her skirt, forcing the drab, salt-stiffened material into wide pleats. 'So I didn't notice… simply didn't notice…'

She broke off, shaking.

'I can do this,' I remember telling myself. 'If Hugo can hear their stories to the end, then so can I.' I even prompted her. 'You didn't notice the wave? You were too busy with your daughter to see it banking up?'

She stared at me as if, until I broke her train of thought, she hadn't realised I was in the cabin. I suddenly understood why Hugo kept saying, 'You're only there to *listen*'. I'd thrown her off her stride. She frowned.

There was the most horrible silence until, at last, she picked up her story. 'I didn't notice the water being sucked away. The sand was changing in texture beneath my feet and I didn't notice that. No, nor the sudden quiet, or that the sea birds were gone. I was so irritated with Elida, I didn't notice a thing. Finally, I must have heard shouting, and looked behind. But it was too late by then. The water was rushing in much faster than I could drag my daughter up the beach, and she was torn away from me. Just torn away! She had a look of such astonishment, as if she couldn't believe I was so angry with her that I would hurl her into rushing water as a punishment.' The woman trembled. 'That's what she thought! I know that's what she thought. I know my child. I know her all too well. She's stubborn and she won't forgive me, won't forgive me, *ever*. She thinks I threw her in the wave and let her go, tumbling over and over until...'

Again, she stopped. Tugging her skirt free, she rose and stared at me for just a moment, then hurried out of the cabin.

I was appalled. I saw the scene that she'd described so vividly I could have been there. It was like all the times I'd pictured the car as it smashed into Toby. I'd had the image of that moment so crystal clear in my brain, so often, that I was astonished to learn, after the coroner's inquest, that the car stolen by James Harper was metallic blue, and not, as I had always seen it, bright, bright red.

As soon as that first grieving mother was gone I scrambled to my feet, unnerved enough to want to get outside. But even before I'd reached the cabin door an elderly man on crutches was pushing his way through it. I hesitated, but I didn't dare try to edge past him. I just sat down again, and pointed to the sofa. The man took time to settle, fussing about with the crutches until he finally gave up and dropped them with a clatter to the floor. The whole time, he was muttering in his own language, sounding so angry that I began to feel even more rattled.

In desperation, I pointed to the kettle. 'Hot drink?'

He shook his head, and started talking louder. I knew that he was talking to me, that much was obvious, but I couldn't understand. He didn't notice – that, or he didn't care. He just kept on with his tale. He talked for what seemed ages. I could tell when he was explaining things. I could guess when he was remembering. I knew for certain when he was most upset because, in spite of what Hugo had told me about the way these people kept their feelings to themselves, the tears rolled down his cheeks. But I had no idea at all what he was saying, except that, as he came towards the end, his eyes locked on to mine. Slowly he counted on his fingers, and it was clear that, with each finger, he was telling me the name of someone he had lost.

Nine of them. Presumably all drowned. And he was left – lame, old and probably alone in the world.

I can't remember who was next. Even that first day quickly became a blur of those relentless voices. Some seemed to be telling me they'd scrambled up the ridge, only to turn and watch their friends and family swept up and tossed into the chaos. Some had seen fishing boats that were carrying their fathers and brothers sucked under the oily black rising wave, then spat up in pieces. One tall, emaciated, ragged man refused to move from the doorway, glancing out every few seconds as if to check the waves he could no longer trust had crept no further up the beach. He, like so many of the rest, came out with his sorry tale in a mix of languages. Still, like the others, at a certain point he seemed to feel he'd said enough – at least for the moment. He stopped short, gave me a hurried nod and rushed down the cabin steps.

And it went on like that.

We fell into a fairly steady routine. By the time Hugo and I walked down to the cabins each morning, at least one person would be waiting – sometimes three or four. I never knew if the Endlanders worked on some sort of system of 'first come, first served', or if they had some other way to decide which of them would go wandering off, and which would follow me or Hugo up the steps.

I always took the cabin with the ropey sofa. Some of the younger ones couldn't help moving around the whole time they were talking, picking up sheets of paper only to stare at them blindly, putting them down again almost at once; fingering the handles of the cabinets; endlessly fidgeting. I totally forgot some of the people almost the moment they left. But if they'd spoken so that I could understand them, it was much harder, afterwards, to put their stories out of my mind. Even if I'd been trying not to pay attention, I'd catch the words, 'ripped from my arms', or, 'saw them swept away', or, 'held on as long as I could', or, 'too strong for me', and even though everyone who came was essentially telling the very same story, bits of those stories stuck.

Mum was in touch a lot. Each time we spoke, she

asked a heap of questions it was hard to bat away. But since I'd not been straight with her in our first calls, it somehow ended up being too late to confess. 'Louie, it sounds the most *peculiar* way of being helpful. You just let people talk to you about their previous lives? Are you sure that you've got it right?'

'That's about it.'

'And they keep at it, even though they know that you don't understand their language?'

By then I'd picked up more of it than you might think, but all I said to Mum was, 'Well, I've got pretty good at saying "Please" and "Thank you".'

'It's just *bizarre*. And I am worried about it. I'm going to check with your dad.'

I don't know what he said. Perhaps he left her with the feeling that, if I wasn't to be scalded by a clumsy volunteer cook, or electrocuted by some poorly trained apprentice, this was a sensible choice. And Dad did ask me more than once, 'You're *sure* that you don't understand whatever it is they're saying?'

I'd fobbed him off, telling him cheerfully, 'Totally over my head.'

I didn't *want* to tell Dad how things really were. (I'd had enough of moping up and down the beach during those first two days.) But it was different with Hugo. 'What is the *point*?' I asked him irritably once, when he came in to snatch me away for soup and sandwiches. 'Why do they need to *do* this? Why would they want to come back, day after day, to tell a perfect stranger who can't understand a word they're saying exactly how these deaths happened?'

I think his leg must have been giving him trouble because he hesitated before stepping over the stream of water running down the sand. 'I've *told* you.' He tried to soothe me. 'It's their *culture*. We might lay flowers on a grave on anniversaries and special days, and they do this. It's how they go about soothing the restless spirits of the ones they love. They tell the story of the loss over and over. The spirit's listening, and is supposed to gradually be calmed by seeing the family's grief, and knowing those who survive are full of sorrow to see them go.'

'They'd know that anyway,' I said, thinking of Toby. 'And I still think it's strange that they would want to rabbit on and on about how it happened. I tell you, if *I* lost a brother—'

I broke off, suddenly aware that Hugo had once again stopped in his tracks. Now he was staring at me. 'Louie?' He laid a hand on my arm. 'Louie, you *have* lost a brother. Your father said he died only a few months ago.'

'Yes. Toby,' I admitted. 'He was run over.'

I could almost hear Hugo thinking, *Then surely you, of all people...* But he said nothing. He just kept on watching.

I tried to defend myself. 'Okay,' I said. 'My brother's dead. It was a horrible accident that no one expected. That much is the same. But I don't spend my time going on and on to other people about the way he died. I try not to think about it any more, because it's too awful. That car must have *smashed* into Toby.' I don't know what got into me, but I couldn't stop, and out came something that I'd never said to anyone. 'Will Hutchin's mother told him she saw a woman tip all of her shopping out into the gutter so she could lay the bag on Toby's head till someone else could cover him better.' My voice rose. 'I don't want to think about that! Why would I? All I want to think about is how unfair it was, and how many foul and awful people in the world it should have happened to instead of Toby! I'll think about how much I miss him, and how much I want him back, and how I know exactly what he'd say if he were here right now, and stuff like that. But I try not to think about exactly how he died! That's horrible! And what's the point of telling someone who's never even *met* your daughter or your grandchild or your husband about the moment when some massive wave swept them away? It would be far more sensible to try to put the whole terrible business behind you and just get on with things.'

'Like you do?'

'Yes,' I snapped back, furious. 'Like *I* do.'

Tears spurted, and I swung away.

TWENTY-SIX

A healing purpose

He sent for Dad, of course. But Dad was at the far end of the bay, behind the mounds of leftover building materials, constructing some sort of gravel chute. So, Hugo sat with me, back in the cabin. I didn't want to speak to him, and made that obvious, so after handing me a cup of sickly sugared tea, he ushered the waiting people along the beach to his own cabin, and left me alone.

'Don't vanish,' were his last words. 'Your dad will be here any moment, and he won't want to have to go and look for you.'

I tipped the tea down the tin sink and made another cup that had no sugar at all. I can't say it was like the tea at home, or even like the stuff that we were given up at the trestle tables. But it was hot and soothing, and I drank it. Then I went out. Already I could see another woman heading my way, but I ignored her. Walking straight past, I went towards the water, which was sparkling cheerfully, as if to tell me to buck up and get a grip.

I thought about how rude I'd been to Hugo about Malouy, calling it stupid and creepy and pointless. I still thought that was true. But once or twice I'd had the sense that something about it might serve a healing purpose. The first time one woman came, she'd talked so fast that I was pretty sure I wouldn't have grasped a word of what she said, even if I'd been fluent in the language. Her face was colourless, as if she had no blood in her at all. She almost might have been made of glass. It was unnerving just to look at her – glass face, glass lips, writhing glass hands.

Next time she came, she sounded a whole lot calmer. She still looked horribly pale, but that strange bloodless look was gone. And then, a few days later, when she came back, she could have been a different woman. She went through her story one more time, firmly and carefully, like someone who had learned their lesson pat, and knew they'd got it right. And then, as she stood up, she gave me a proper smile and turned at the door to give me what

I could tell was not just a final wave, but also a real thank you.

And then there was the old man who said nothing. He came and sat. When I became uncomfortable with the silence, I asked him, 'Do you want to tell your story?', as Hugo had advised.

He shook his head. 'Good lad,' he said. 'Good lad.'

I thought at first he might be speaking of a son or grandchild he had lost. But it was obvious from how he gently patted down the air between us that he was simply asking me to leave him be.

So I sat quietly and waited. Once or twice a tear rolled into one of the deep creases in his face. There was the odd sharp intake of breath as he remembered things. But he said nothing.

In the end he stood up, shook my hand, told me, 'Good lad,' again, and went away. I don't know why I was so sure that sitting there had done him good. But I knew that it had, and next time I saw him working on his nets, he waved at me cheerily across the sand.

But these were two out of many. And even then, I wasn't sure that anything about my being there had really helped. I tried to put the whole peculiar business out of my mind, waiting for Dad. I kicked at the sand

and stared at the incoming waves, wondering if the fishermen still trusted them the way they had before, or if they now had to take courage simply to push their boats out from the shore.

And that's when the next ghosts came – while I was standing at the water's edge, just gazing blankly out over the glittering bay.

One of them touched me. That's why I turned. She'd startled me because, apart from the woman heading for the cabin, no one had been around when I went down to the water. This was a child. She couldn't have been more than six or seven, and she had another, younger, child by the hand. The two of them looked so alike that it was obvious they were sisters. And they were sopping wet, standing there in bare feet, with torn clothes, tangled hair and filthy faces. I knew at once that they were ghosts.

The air around suddenly seemed curiously still. All I could do was wait. And finally, the elder one said something in the local language.

'Sorry?'

This time she spoke so I could understand. 'We're looking for the causeway. Where is the causeway?'

'The causeway?'

That's when my father's voice came ringing down the beach. 'Lou-*ie!*' I turned to shout, 'Coming!', and when I looked back, both of the girls had gone. They'd vanished into the sunlight, leaving two small damp patches in the sand.

I ran back up the beach. 'Did you see that?'

'That boat of tourists? Yes. I wish they wouldn't sail into the bay simply to gawp.'

He hadn't, then. If he had seen the girls, he would have seen them vanish. But I kept quiet. Dad probably already thought that I was on the edge. Hugo was bound to have explained about my losing it and bursting into tears. That's why Dad had shown up, after all. I didn't want him thinking this trip was all too much for me so soon after Toby's death. He would have sent me home. So, I walked back with him without a word to stand in front of the unfolding waves.

I don't think Dad was very sure what to say, either. He stared down at the ripples in the sand, pushing up clumsy ridges with the side of his work boot. 'So, Louie, Hugo says that everything has got to you suddenly.'

Instantly, Toby showed up in my brain. 'Bit harsh,' I heard him say, in that old joking tone of his. 'Not everyone can see a brace of ghosts and not flip out.'

I nearly told him, 'Sshh!' before I turned to Dad. 'Is that what Hugo told you?' But then I realised there was no point in denying it. 'It has. It really has.'

'Anything in particular?'

He was the last one I'd be able to tell. How could he bear it either? Toby was his *son*. I gave another reason. 'I think it's probably because I just can't see the point. Why would they think it helps, just going on like that?' Before he could interrupt, I warned him irritably, 'And please don't spoon out Hugo's line that this is "cultural". So were rain dances. And reading chickens' entrails. All sorts of stupid stuff. If these people want to waste their time among themselves, then fair enough. That is their business. But I feel stupid sitting there when I could be doing something useful. I could be helping *you*.'

That's when the echo of my brother's voice broke in on me again. 'Hey, Louie! How come you're so snitty about what they're doing? What about you? You might not talk *about* me all the time. But you still talk *to* me.'

That shook me – not so much his uninvited voice, since I was getting used to that – but what he said. I did have to admit he had a point. If everyone round here was in some curious no man's land from losing somebody, then so was I. Their ghosts were sometimes visible. Mine was a voice in my head. But none of them were fully laid to rest. However it arrives, death is the most sudden thing. One moment you're alive, the next you're not. But grief is long. So long. These people on the bay had always had this way of managing it. Every last person who came through that cabin door was sure in his or her mind that, grim as the story of that death might be, this was the way to ease a troubled spirit. It's what they'd always done, and they believed it worked. And, to be fair, it was a definite echo of what the counsellor at school had wanted me to do – to talk to someone about Toby.

But I hadn't been honest with my dad or Valentina about what was going on. And though Hugo had often taken care to remind me that if even the mere idea of what they might be saying began to get to me, I had to take a break and come and talk to him, I'd never done that. We'd started with a sort of distance between us, almost as if he had been one of my teachers in school, and I admit that I preferred to let things stay that way. Some of the other volunteers would make remarks about what we were doing down in the cabins. 'It sounds so *weird.*' But Hugo always had an answer. 'Other people's customs always seem odd. But mostly, unless you have a very good reason, it's best to treat them with respect.'

And something about the self-righteous way he said it did tend to send them back to talking about other things. So I never ended up, even by accident, letting it drop that, though the people who came to Hugo's cabin might speak in their own language, they didn't always when they were in mine.

And did it matter? Because, if I'm honest, even when I could understand what they were saying, I very often did stop listening and let my thoughts drift off. Most of the stories were pretty much the same, after all. The wave came. They lost someone, or several people, they had loved. Only the way the story was told was different every time. Endlanders talking and me listening. But I thought of Toby a lot. So maybe, I thought, standing there letting the white wavelets roll towards me and splinter into lacy patterns round my soaking trainers, it wasn't quite so mad as I had thought. And maybe not so pointless.

Dad stood beside me, staring at the water. I got the feeling he was turning something over in his own mind, more than deciding what to say to me. Was he, too, thinking of Toby? Dad kept his feelings so locked up that it was hard to ask. But then he put an arm around my shoulders to steer me up the beach. 'No problem, Louie. I can find something else for you to do.'

I pulled myself together. 'No, not just yet. I'd rather try to carry on. Can't we tell Hugo it was just a little wobble?'

'We could. But only if you're sure that's what you want.' He paused. '*Are* you sure? After all, even if you can't understand a word they're saying, you know what they're on about. Valentina is right. It can't be the easiest job for you.' Again, he hesitated. 'I mean, what with Toby . . .'

He'd done it! Said my brother's name! It seemed the moment to come out with what had been preying on my mind from the day we drove back together to the bay. 'Dad, can I ask you something? Does Toby ever...'

'Ever . . .?'

I took a rush at it. 'Does Toby ever get inside your *brain*?'

He didn't know exactly what it was that I was getting at. He clearly hadn't heard the voice the way I had. What he said was, 'Louie, I think about your brother a hundred times a day. More, probably.' He kicked the sand. 'And it's horrible. Just *horrible*. I keep on hoping that some day I'll get to a place in my head where I can think of him with pleasure, as a good-looking and amusing lad who had a short but happy life.' He broke off. For a moment, I thought he'd finished all he had to say. But then he added bitterly, 'Not, like I do now, thinking of him with every cell of me aching, all day and every day, because it was *too* short a life.'

I couldn't help it. I stopped in my tracks. I was so angry, wondering if he had even the faintest idea how very *dense* he had been. 'Why haven't you *said* it, then?' I challenged him. 'Why have you gone on, all this time, not saying anything, just keeping all the horrid things you're feeling to yourself? Why didn't you come out with any of it before? It could have helped *so much*. Things might have been all right! You should have said it, Dad! And *months* ago!' I honestly think I must have been shouting at him. 'You really should have said it!'

He stared at me, his face red, and stretched out a hand to lay it on my arm. But I stepped back. I wouldn't let him touch me. I was furious. And in the end, he said, 'I am so sorry, Louie. If I'd had even the slightest notion that it would have helped, I would have said something to you.'

Now I was even madder. 'Stupid! It was so *stupid* not to say something! And not to me! That's not what I'm talking about! You should have said it all to *Mum*.'

TWENTY-SEVEN

And that will be never

I went back to the job that I'd been given. For nearly another whole week I sat in that cramped cabin, listening. I tried to let pretty much everything I heard wash over me, whether or not I understood what the person was saying. Oh, I could nod, and make the odd encouraging 'keep going' noise. But mostly I'd be miles away, thinking about what I would say to Will about my weeks on the bay when I got back, or about what Mum might be doing at home, or anything she and I might have talked about last time we spoke. I thought about the fast-approaching school term, and which sport to choose for Wednesday afternoons. I thought about the films I hoped I'd still have time to see before the holidays were over. Odd, drifting stuff like that. Sometimes I thought about Toby. But not, unlike those I was supposed to be listening to, about the way he died. Why should I want to think about whether or not my brother actually saw the car coming and suddenly realised for sure that it was going to hit him? Or how much that moment hurt? Instead, I thought about things like how strange it was for Toby to have, at one moment, a past, a present and a future – just like everybody else. And the next moment, only to have a past.

I thought a lot about that past. I thought about the things that I myself remembered. Not just the good times, or the times when I was really grateful to him for sticking up for me at school. I thought back on our quarrels and his occasional little meannesses. I thought about the stiff little gathering at our house straight after the funeral, when Will and I, and Toby's best friend, Jimmy St George, were all in suits, and what I'd heard when most of my parents' friends had tactfully gone home, and the only ones left were the relations who'd come from miles away. Someone who claimed she was my great-aunt Jessica had reached for the last cheese sandwich on a plate at the same time as I did, then drew back her hand. 'Go ahead, Louie.'

'No, thanks,' I said. 'I didn't really want it anyway.'

I thought she'd press me to take it, but she didn't.

She picked it up and took a bite. 'I'm starving. My flight got in so late this morning that I had to run for the connecting train.'

It'd seemed only polite to ask her, 'Where were you coming from?'

'Egypt.'

'*Egypt?*'

She gave me a bit of a look. 'I was extremely fond of your mother when she was a child. I know I've barely been in contact for years. But a son is a son. And he was very young indeed.'

I asked, 'When you last saw him?' before I realised that she must have meant 'very young to have died'.

'That too,' she said. 'He can't have been much more than two. I know you were exactly five months old.'

'You remember that?'

'I do.' She smiled. 'Because the little devil kept rolling you over. You had a brightly coloured mat to lie on. It had arches over it, with things hanging from clips. Baby stuff – furry koalas, rattles, balls on elastic, jingling bells. That sort of thing. I don't remember exactly, but your mother did tell me you'd only just learned to roll yourself over so you could reach for them. And there was Tobias—'

'*Tobias?*'

Great Aunt Jessica looked at me gravely. 'I think you'll find that's the name on his birth certificate.'

'Really?'

She brushed my disbelief away. 'If you doubt me, just go and ask your mother.' Hastily, she added the warning, 'But not *today*.'

We stood together while she ate the rest of the sandwich she'd been holding all this time and I wondered if my brother's brand new death certificate had got him down as a proper Tobias, or just the Toby I knew. After a moment, Great Aunt Jessica went back to what she'd been saying. 'He kept on rolling you over. Whichever way you wanted to be – on your back or your tummy – he kept on flipping you the other way. Your mother must have ticked him off for it a hundred times while I was sitting there. I wonder that she didn't lose her patience.'

I didn't say it but, thinking about what Dad always called 'your mother's rather impatient streak', I wondered at that, too.

'Anyhow,' she said, 'I must go off and say goodbye to her, or I shall miss my flight home.'

'You've only come for the *day*?'

She gave me yet another of those looks. It seemed as if she might be about to launch into some sort of Mum-like ticking off herself. But in the end she only said, 'Louie, I didn't come 'for the day'. Like everyone else who's been inside this house this afternoon, I came for your parents. And for you.'

After she'd gone, I looked round at the people standing there so uneasily in their dark suits or dresses, all looking so unhappy, and couldn't help remembering what Will had said when I'd gone into school two days before, to pick up the homework. 'My dad says funeral parties can sometimes be good fun, but that your brother's will be grim from start to finish because no one can bear it when young people die.'

My own dad had already made it clear that anyone who tried to take a cheery line on things would not be welcome. 'I've had to phone just about everyone to warn them,' he'd told me. 'Your mother says if she sees anyone wearing bright colours because they think that "Toby would have liked it", she's going to throw them out. She says she isn't up for anybody trying to celebrate your brother's life till she's done mourning his death.' He didn't add that Mum had finished up, even more bitterly, 'And that will be bloody *never*.' But

I'd been there, behind the door, and I had heard her.

Mum wasn't even trying to smile politely now. She was just standing, stiff as stone, as people said goodbye, and tried to pat her arm, or offered feebly to stay and help clear up. She didn't even thank them. And even before Dad shooed out the last few stragglers ('Get *rid* of them, Phil! Please! Tell them they have to *go*!') she went upstairs and cried for hours and hours.

So, it was days before we'd had the conversation. 'Was Toby really called Tobias?'

She stared at me as if I'd asked her if my brother had been born on the moon. It was a good few seconds before the fairly simple question sank in. 'Well, yes. You've seen his passport, surely?'

'The photo, yes. But maybe he always took great care to keep his thumb over the name bit.'

'He certainly refused to answer to anything except Toby.' She looked at me, still baffled, before asking, 'So who on earth mentioned that?'

'That lady who said she was our Great Aunt Jessica.'

(I realised it was now '*my* Great Aunt Jessica', but didn't see how I could backtrack to correct it.)

'Oh, *Jess*. I must say I was startled she came all this way. But it was really good of her to make the effort.

I don't believe she'd ever even seen Toby.'

'She says she did. When I was five months old. She said she spent an afternoon with you, and Toby kept rolling me over on my mat.'

'Did he? Oh, yes. Now I remember. He used to do that a lot.'

'So was he jealous of me? Was he being mean?'

'No, not at all. It's just that, right from when you were tiny, your brother seemed to think you were some special toy he was allowed to play with.'

'A *toy*?'

She tried to explain. 'Yes. You were supposed to fit in with whatever he wanted to play. Even when you were in your cot, he used to play a game called Hungry Prisoner. He'd be the jailer, and feed you stuff through the bars.'

'What stuff?'

She shrugged. 'Small bits of biscuit. Strips of buttered toast. Anything I'd let him give you.'

'So you were in on all this?'

She gave me a smile. It was a bit watery, but it was still a smile. 'Louie,' she said, 'one day you'll learn that parents will do almost anything to keep small children happy.'

Right then, the doorbell rang. As usual now, Mum stepped back out of sight of anyone who might peep through the window. 'Louie, you go.' But by the time I reached the door, whoever had pressed the bell had vanished and another casserole dish was on the step.

I carried it into the kitchen. 'The note says it's *chilli con carne.*'

We both knew that was Toby's favourite.

Mum said, with the steadiest voice that she could manage, 'We've too much food already. I'll find something else to put it in, and shove it in the freezer.'

She sent me back to the Woodruffs' with the clean casserole dish and a thank-you note the very next morning. But I don't remember us eating *chilli con carne* ever again.

TWENTY-EIGHT

They're not exactly *there*, are they?

Fresh sea air makes you hungry. By the time one of the volunteer cooks came out to clang the handbell in the evenings to signal that the food was on the tables, I was usually first in the queue. I couldn't wait. Mornings were different. Sometimes I would have loved to have stayed lazing on my bunk. But Dad did seem to like my company at meals, and on the days he didn't push off early, I'd join him for breakfast in spite of the fact that he would almost always raise the same old worry. 'You're *sure* that you're not listening to all these awful tales?'

I'd bat the question away. 'But that's exactly what I'm there to do, isn't it?'

'You know what I mean. You're sure that you're not understanding what they say? You've been here nearly three weeks. You must have picked up at least a bit of the language.'

I thought I'd better admit that I was well beyond just knowing how to say 'please' and 'thank you'. 'I recognise the word "Greetings". And, "Thank you for listening to my story". And I hear people say "*Spi Ruaradh*" quite a lot.'

'*Spi Ruaradh*? Why would they talk about *Spi Ruaradh*?'

'It was supposed to be a sacred place, remember?'

I didn't tell him I'd been tempted to ask why it came up so much, but Hugo's endless reminders that I was supposed only to listen had stopped me interrupting anyone with questions.

'Great mysteries of other people's cultures,' he said, and, shoving the last bit of toast into his mouth, he rose from the table. 'Well, just so long as you're okay.'

He went off. I hung about, hoping more bacon would show up. Over the last few days I hadn't been hurrying along to the cabin straight after breakfast the way I had before because the number of people showing up was thinning out a lot. I couldn't tell if those who'd come had found me useless, so chose to wait for a turn with Hugo instead, or if their way of calming their unhappy spirits was actually working. But sometimes when I looked out no one at all was waiting. I'd wander off along the bay, looking for Dad. None of the projects he and Valentina were involved with seemed to be anything like as urgent as before, and Dad would often take a break. We'd go and sit a short way up the ridge. Sometimes he took a nap. Sometimes we talked. We never had another conversation like the one we'd had before. But I did notice that now, whenever I brought my brother's name up, my dad no longer flinched, or acted deaf. It was a whole lot easier to talk to him, knowing that I no longer had to watch for where the conversation might be going.

One time, when he was sprawled out on his back, chewing a stalk of grass, eyes closed against the sun, I even dared to ask, 'Will you and Mum get back together, do you think?'

'Oh, yes,' he said, with no hesitation at all. 'We definitely will.'

'Really?'

'No doubt about it. And all thanks to you.'

At first, I didn't get it. 'Why? Because I'm still at school?'

He barely opened his eyes as he reached out to ruffle

my hair. 'No, idiot. Because you made me say the name Toby out loud again.'

I asked, astonished, 'Have you been talking about this to Mum?'

'Of course.'

'What, *often*?'

'Most days,' he admitted, a little guiltily.

'What else do you talk about?'

Already, he had scrambled to his feet. 'Mind your own business, Louie.' He reached down to pull me up. His arm went round my shoulder until the narrow path forced us apart. And I can remember feeling as safe as when he used to come upstairs at night and tuck me and Toby into our beds so firmly we could barely wriggle free again.

Really. That safe.

One morning, Dad was nowhere to be found. I checked to see if anyone had come to wait outside the cabin while I was looking for him, then set off on my own along the beach. I reached the water channel and made the usual jump, but this time one foot slid back into the water, which was swirling down faster and deeper than before.

I looked up to where the stream tumbled down

the gully, rippling silver. Its path down the ridge now looked a good deal wider than I remembered. Was this, I wondered, the water that seeped round our shoes when we'd had to jump on to the fallen boulders at the pumping station? No longer pumped off to Topane, could it be gathering underground and rising somewhere underneath the ridge, spilling out here on the beach?

Julia might know, but I had no idea. I stamped the damp sand from my heel and kept on walking, further than before. Bright clouds slid overhead, and where there were clumps of rocks along the shoreline, spray from the breaking waves cooled my hot face. Distracted by the echoes of some sea shanty which I'd learned back in primary school, I suddenly realised that the sound of it was actually coming from me. I was singing at the top of my voice.

I realised, for the first time in months, that I was *happy*.

That's when I spotted Dad, coming the other way.

'Did you go right to the end?' I asked, once he was near enough. I pointed. 'Around that headland?'

'No, I only went as far as the old burial ground.'

I looked along the beach. All I could see were

stretches of white sand. 'Where's that?'

Dad waved an arm towards some clumps of scrub grass pockmarking the bottom of the ridge. 'Just along there. Hugo said where to look for it. He wanted to know if any of the shrines had been replaced, and it's too far for his bad leg, so I said that I'd stroll along and look.'

I stared at the thin, waving grasses. 'I can't see anything. But then again, if no one's died round here since the tsunami washed the place away, why would they bother?'

'Somewhere to sit and mourn?' He saw my doubting look. 'I mean, even if all their ancestors' memorials were swept out to sea, they must still need a place to go to try and conjure up the ghosts of those they've lost.'

I thought about the dripping figures Mrs Henderson and I had seen, and he and Valentina never had. 'You think they actually *try* to conjure them?'

'So Hugo says.' Then Dad astonished me by adding, 'And when you think about it, it makes sense. Maybe they only see these things in the first place because they want to so much. Hugo suggests that maybe they as good as *insist* on the spirits of their lost ones coming back because they miss them so badly.' He shrugged. 'I mean, they're not exactly *there*, are they?'

I understood that. It was, I thought, like me and Toby. If it was Toby-not-exactly-there, or Toby-not-at-all, I knew which I would choose. Why would you be unnerved or anxious if the one you loved, and lost so suddenly, was there, but only in spirit? When someone dies, you see them all around in any case. I've seen my brother vanishing round every corner in school. I've seen his face in almost every crowded street. I've even seen his eyes staring at me out of puddles.

Now Dad had turned to gaze out over the still blue water. And what he said next really startled me. It wasn't at all like him, and I suspected suddenly that he had spent a good deal more time talking to Hugo than I had ever guessed. He said, 'It's probably all some of the living ever want – to see their dead again. And if their bodies are out there in the water, so they can't even hold a proper funeral, maybe their whole lives turn into an act of mourning.'

Again, I thought of Toby. He'd had a proper funeral, with everything – music and silence and tears and memories. Mostly, of course, his body in its glossy wicker coffin, studded with flowers.

He did have that, at least.

We did have that.

We walked on. After a while, Dad said, 'I'm sorry I'll have nothing to report. I quite like the idea of shrines.' Since he was clearly still in a more than usually thoughtful mood, with Toby close to mind, he added, 'Do you remember the pair of you jumping over those graves in Italy? Getting told off by that fierce old widow when Toby knocked over a photo of her husband.'

'And her ending up giving us those horrible dry biscuits, and hugging Mum.'

'Those graves were sorts of shrines, with all those photos and flowers and small mementos on the top.' He pointed back to just beyond where I'd met him. 'Lavish, compared to any of the scattered bits and pieces I saw up there. But Hugo told me there's no early history of burial grounds round here. He thinks, until this washed-out graveyard was set up, the Endlanders must have had some other, much more hidden, way of dealing with their dead.'

I said, 'So if there was nothing back there, maybe they've given up on that place?'

He nodded. 'Gone back to doing things in some much older way.' The shadow of a cloud swept up the wastes of sand and suddenly the beach seemed very bleak. 'He says they never wanted any burial ground in the first place, and when the plans for it were first put forward, there was the strongest resistance. Only directives from the central government forced the decision through.' He shrugged. 'Frankly, I would have thought they would have liked it here, so close to the water. What was it Valentina said about the people on this bay? That they have always seemed to belong more to the sea than the land.'

We walked back quietly together and, just as we were going past the cabins, one of the army engineers I'd often seen working with Dad nodded his way. 'Good walk, Phil? Did you and the boys get all the way to the far end?'

Dad looked a little baffled. 'Boys?'

She smiled, and waved at me. 'Yes, this one, and the other who was walking along behind you. The one who'd been in the water and was *dripping* wet.'

TWENTY-NINE

Get back to life

That night I dreamed that Toby met me in the changing rooms at school. '*Was* that you on the beach?' I'd asked. 'Or some drowned boy of theirs?'

He'd grinned in the old, teasing way. 'You want to watch it, Louie, or you might go bats.'

Then, walking away through the foot bath between the changing rooms and pool, he'd vanished.

I'd laid awake for hours, and when morning finally came, I must have shrugged off Dad's usual gentle shaking, or been so deeply asleep that he'd decided to leave me lying there in peace.

I heard the bell, though – the one that's rung loudly enough to warn late sleepers they have only minutes left to get some breakfast. I was up and dressed in a flash. Bolting down eggs, I saw Dad hurrying back along the beach. He clambered in beside me on the bench, making it wobble. 'So? Have you heard anything?'

I'd no idea what he was talking about. 'Heard anything about what?'

'Valentina.' He waved a hand towards the last few volunteers at the far end of the table. 'I thought they might have found out why she'd gone.'

'I didn't know she had.'

'I didn't either. I've just been told that she left suddenly last night.'

'Perhaps there was some problem back at home.'

'Perhaps.' Dad seemed uneasy. 'But I've a feeling it was something here. All I've been told is that the firm had sent her over to the pumping station. She was supposed to supervise the job of making it safe.'

I thought about the state that it was in when we last saw it. 'Safe?'

'Fit to abandon.' Without even thinking, he picked up one of the pieces of toast I'd just buttered. 'There are strict rules about closing down a work plant, however far out in the sticks it happens to be.' He waved the toast at me in warning fashion. 'Louie, you just can't underestimate how stupid people can be, nosing round ruined places. And even if some halfwit does nothing more than graze a finger, someone they know will still encourage them to start a massive court case.'

'So, what do you have to do? Replace the fencing?'

'That's just the start. Last week, they brought in heavy equipment to fetch down any last sections of wall that might collapse on trespassers. And Valentina would have been responsible for checking the site for sharps and toxics. But now it seems she's done a runner. Somehow she managed to blag a seat out on last night's helicopter.' He frowned with either irritation or concern. 'Oh, well. I suppose she'll be in touch soon enough to explain.'

'I suppose so.'

'You'll keep your ears pinned back?'

'I will.'

Dad took one last piece of toast away with him, back to whatever he was doing. I eavesdropped on the volunteers, but they were talking about nothing in particular, so I lost interest and wandered off towards my cabin.

Once again, no one was waiting. And no one came all morning. I kicked about a bit, bored stiff, and envying Valentina her escape, and in the end gave up and walked to Hugo's cabin. When his most recent customer had drifted off, I poked my head round the door. 'I know why no one comes to my place any more,' I said. 'They've finally worked out that I'm a rubbish listener.'

He took my remark as if I'd been deadly serious. 'Don't beat yourself up, Louie. I've only got a few still coming myself. We should be pleased. It shows that almost all of them believe it's been working.'

I tried to nod as if I agreed with him. But, frankly, I wasn't as pleased as he was about the locals thinking their family's restless spirits might be happier. The listening business still seemed peculiar to me, and though I couldn't say as much to Hugo, I was just glad I wouldn't have to hear so many awful stories of coffins bursting from the ground and rising with the water, only to splinter open and spew out bones. Or sit through so many grim accounts of house walls splitting as easily as if they'd been made from paper, and precious sons and daughters being sucked out along with all the furniture, then hurled back in again, their bodies broken, then sucked out again, only to disappear. I'd had enough of pain and misery and loss. I wanted to get back to life.

Hugo kept on. 'I'm glad it's almost over, too. I've

found it quite a strain, and I'm a counsellor. And even though you've not understood what they've been saying, you must have found it difficult.'

There was no point in putting Hugo straight on that – not after all this time. So I just said, 'I'm glad that there was something I could do, what with my Dad and Valentina not letting me do any real work.'

He gave me one of those looks that would have come along with a pat on the head if I'd been five years younger. 'Louie, you're selling yourself short. You *have* worked – very hard.' That set him thinking, and he glanced both ways along the beach. 'Look, no one's coming. Why don't I hold the fort? You bunk off for the day. Do something cheerful.'

He must have seen my look of doubt that there was anything truly cheerful to do on Causeway Bay. 'Go climb the ridge,' he suggested. 'Take a few photos of the view before you go back home.'

I went off, wishing for the hundredth time I was allowed to swim. The endless sparkle of soft waves along the bay made the idea so tempting. But Dad and Valentina had insisted there were slicks of oil and chemicals still in the water, and I'd heard one of the volunteers claiming that rotting bodies still washed up from time to time. I wasn't sure that I believed what she had said. Still, there was no way I was going to take the chance.

Nor did I really fancy climbing the ridge. Instead, as usual when I was bored, I went to look for Dad. Even if he didn't knock off work to spend time with me, I liked to watch him at whatever he was doing. It was a bit like being at home, seeing him struggle with a seized bolt, or twisting rusted parts off something he was trying to fix. It made me feel as if I was almost back to being safe in my old family, even if everything around us was not a part of our real life, and Toby was still gone.

This time, I tracked him down to what everyone called 'the bits and pieces shed'.

'I'm looking for a pair of grip-lock pliers,' he explained when I showed up. 'Someone's made off with mine.' He looked up from the heap of tools he had been rooting through. 'So, Louie. Free again?'

'No customers. I reckon Hugo thinks the listening job is pretty well done.'

'Really? I still see a good few locals on the beach most nights, doing the old routine – what's that it's called.'

'Malouy?'

'That's it.'

'How do you know that's what they're doing?' I asked, and had a further thought. 'And when are you out on the beach at night?'

'I see them on my way to the toilet block.' Dad went back to pushing tools aside, still searching. 'Wait till you're my age. Young sprigs like you roll over and stay dead to the world till morning. Oldies like me are doomed to toss and turn, and then decide we have to get up for another pee.'

I hadn't realised. I'd heard footsteps often enough, and the click of the door latch – even felt drifts of cool and salty air float past my bunk. But there were others in the hut apart from us, and I'd assumed that it was always one of them creeping in late at night, not my own father creeping out.

'Maybe they're back to telling their stories mostly to one another.'

'Who knows? But lots of them gather most nights at the far end of the beach. There's usually enough moonlight to see them, and once or twice it's even been chilly enough for them to build a small fire.'

I can't explain, but suddenly I was infuriated. It was as if all of the weeks that I'd been listening to this stuff had just been a waste of time. 'Why won't they *stop*? How come they've never have *enough*? I mean, imagine if—'

I stopped dead. There was no way that I was going to finish that out loud. But Dad guessed anyway. 'I've often thought that, Louie. I think, if either you or your mother started going on and on, over and over, about how...' He, too, broke off. 'Well, thank God that's not going to happen.'

He turned back to the tools. I stood and watched, wondering if what he'd said might be the first small clue to why he'd been the way he was all those past months. Why he'd not been prepared to talk about my brother, or, for so long, so much as say his name. Why, since that terrible moment when Toby's coffin was raised at the end of the funeral, he'd never even howled aloud with grief.

Why he had battened down the hatches and just kept busy, busy, busy.

Why he had stayed out here.

Maybe he'd got it wrong – shared so few of his feelings that Mum had reached breaking point. But everyone has to try to protect themselves in their own way. What would have been the point in Dad trying to get through all that driving pain in any way that wouldn't work for him? He would have ended up destroyed. He would have turned into another crippling source of pain for everyone around him – stopped being calm and sensible, dependable Dad and added yet another layer of loss and misery to Mum's deep grief.

What was so wrong with trying to stay strong? We weren't Endlanders. We weren't tall and pale. We didn't stare unblinkingly at strangers. And we did not belong more to the sea than the land. Not me, or Dad, or Mum. That wasn't our way at all.

I'd had enough of Causeway Bay and everything to do with it. I almost wished I'd never come. I just burst out with it. 'Can we go home now, please?'

He gave up rooting in the pile. 'Go home?'

'Yes. *Home*. Miles did. And so has Valentina. Hugo can manage without me, and even you've admitted that you're coming to the end of being useful.'

He didn't brush the whole idea away. He stood there, mulling it over just the same way that he would have done if Toby had asked if he could go on a camping trip with mates, or I'd said that I needed my allowance early. At last, he made up his mind. 'These people are still in a mess,' he said. 'You only have to look around to see that. But there's no doubt the worst is over. And there are plenty of skilled volunteers still offering to come.'

'So, can we go? Because I'm *so* fed up with it.'

The way I'd put it startled even me. It sounded silly and childish – especially after all the fuss I'd made to join him in the first place. I added hastily, 'Not fed up with stupid things like boring food, and sleeping on that smelly bed roll. Not even with the business of trying to be helpful.' Suddenly I knew quite clearly what it was I'd found most difficult about my time at the bay. 'It's just, I need to be away from how they *think.*'

'How who think?'

'The Endlanders.' Even though there was no one else about, I realised I was lowering my voice. 'All the things they believe. I mean, I wouldn't have wanted to spend whole weeks listening to people who think they can foretell the future by charting comets, or dabbling in entrails, or feeling bumps on people's heads. I wouldn't have the patience to sit politely listening to people who believe stuff like that. And I'm not sure that I can sit there any longer, hearing them tell the stories of the people they've lost, over and over, till I could tell it back to them, and not get a single awful detail wrong, or out of order.'

I saw the dawning look of horror on my father's face, but I ignored it, pressing on before he could interrupt. 'I know I'm not expected to pretend that I *believe* that there are really restless spirits out there who need calming down.' Deliberately, I pushed all thoughts of Toby aside. 'It comes to much the same thing, though, doesn't it, if I'm just sitting there, endlessly patient, never arguing? *That's* why I want to get away. Doing this job is making me ratty. No. Worse than ratty. *Furious.*' I had the feeling Dad was trying not to smile as I kept on. 'You know for sure that you are being useful. But I am worried I'm just wasting my time and Hugo is wasting his.'

I never thought I'd hear Dad sticking up for anything irrational. He did, though. 'Louie, it works for *them.* And you can *see* it's working, just like, in other places, praying might really, really help someone religious, or starting a charity in a child's name might be a massive comfort.'

I told him sourly, 'It's not like you to shrug and say, "Whatever works".'

He gave a rueful smile. 'I don't know. Any engineer

might start to think that way if they were desperate.' He let out the longest sigh. 'Death is so big. So final. Maybe I have begun to think, "whatever works". And that means Hugo's *not* been wasting his time, and neither have you. Not for a single moment.'

It was a comfort, what he said. But I still felt dead sour. 'Maybe you're right. But it's their culture, not mine, and I have had *enough* of it. I want to go *home*.'

'Home…'

Dad said it almost wonderingly, as if he'd halfway to forgotten that there was such a place. I couldn't see why I shouldn't finish telling him what I was thinking.

'And I don't see why you can't come back with me. You've done your bit. It wasn't *your* fault the tsunami happened while you were working here. That doesn't make you responsible for sorting everything out. You don't have to stay around till every last tiny bit of equipment is working perfectly. Valentina's just done a bunk, and there's no reason you can't decide it's fine for you to bail out too.'

Now Dad was definitely smiling. The worry lines had vanished. There was a broad grin on his face. 'Hell, Louie! Why not? You're right. If we'd not been here when the earthquake came, I wouldn't have downed tools to come and help. I would have done what everybody else does – made a donation to the relief fund, and left the work to all the younger engineers who don't have families and who *want* to travel. I'd have got on with my own life.'

I was so happy. 'So, we can really *go*?'

'Why not?' he said again.

'Can I tell Mum?'

'You better had,' he said, still grinning. 'She didn't thank me last time for turning up at her door with no notice at all.'

I didn't think that he could possibly have misunderstood what had made Mum so angry. Still, I defended her. 'That was because you told her you were going away again almost at once. I know that she'll be really glad if you've come back for good.'

'Right, then,' he said. 'I'll set wheels turning. Checking the Causeway plant is fit to abandon shouldn't take long. I'll make that my very last job.'

That's when I heard it in my brain again, quite unmistakably – my brother's cheerful voice. 'Your last job's there as well, Louie. And once you've done that, we can all go home.'

THIRTY

New ways to be

I was determined not to let the fact that Toby was back unnerve me. Dad and I were going home! He had as good as promised! I watched him give up on his search for grip-lock pliers and set off along the beach with one or two other tools to try to finish whatever it was that he'd been doing. Light-headed with relief, I started up the ridge to get as far as possible from the long bay I almost couldn't wait never to see again. I was so happy.

I didn't even stop halfway to look back down and see if any Endlanders were gathering at the cabins. I didn't want to know. It was as if Dad's saying we could leave so soon had given me permission to shove the listening job right out of my mind.

I just kept scrambling up. Even before I'd come through the narrow belt of trees the tidal wave never reached, I was thinking of home. I longed to see my mum again, and not just on a screen. I knew the day that I got back I'd see Will properly, and even if I still wasn't supposed to tell him everything about the past three weeks, I would have lots to say. There'd still be time, I realised, to get to a couple of the films whose trailers I had seen before I left. Will more than likely would have watched them all already. But maybe he would be prepared to come with me and see them a second time.

Then we'd be back at school. A new year in a different form room. The special option subjects I had chosen. New teachers, even.

A fresh start.

I stepped out from the shadow of the trees, and reached the very last section of the climb, up through thin, waving grasses on the stony ground. And suddenly I was there, right at the top, exactly where we'd been the day the four of us stood in a line, holding our melting ice creams and staring down at trees that floated like toothpicks, at houses that had burst into a thousand pieces, and boats and carts and cars flung all about as if some toddler in a rage had hurled every toy within his reach into the water.

It had looked, then, strangely familiar, like a

computer-generated sequence from any disaster film. The shock had been that I was actually standing there watching. This time, the scene was calm. I could still hear the faint hum of generators constantly strumming their stuff way down below. But mostly there was just the rustle of the wind through grass, and that strange, slightly bitter smell that Valentina had once said she thought was sagebrush.

I found a wide flat rock, and sat on it to think. New school years mean fresh chances. Resolutions. New ways to think about things. New ways to be. And I was well aware I'd changed a lot in the last weeks. For one thing, I felt even more impressed with Mum. She'd always had true grit. No one could live in the same house as her for more than a week without knowing that. But now I'd come to realise how very brave she was. She hadn't tried to stuff Toby's death, or even all our previous life with him, into a box and hide away from it. She'd met it all face on, courageously, like some great warrior going into battle with her head held high.

And Dad. I knew him so much better now. Up till this trip he'd always seemed to me to be more of a fixer of things than a whole person. He'd let Mum lead the way, and been her huge support. But now, I felt, I'd seen him growing out of that protective shell of his. I'd seen inside him for the very first time.

What about me? How had things changed for me?

Well, I was happier. Not anywhere near as happy as I would have been if I still had my brother. I didn't think I'd ever be that happy again. But I was nowhere near as miserable as I'd been since his death. I reckoned I could probably go home and do what Mum and Dad had always told the two of us to do when we were small and we had grazed our knees, or bruised ourselves. Even if it was still hurting horribly. 'Be a brave soldier'.

'Be a *what*?'

Oh, God! Had I actually spoken? I spun round and, sure enough, just a short way behind me Julia Henderson was sitting on another rock, smiling. I had the feeling she'd been there some time.

'Be a brave soldier,' I admitted. 'I can't believe I really said that aloud.'

'You did, though. Shortly after you asked yourself if you were happier now. I certainly hope the answer to that one came out positive.'

'It did,' I said. 'I actually think it did.'

She came to sit beside me on my own rock. 'Bunking off?'

'Saying goodbye to the place,' I told her. 'Dad and I are going home.'

'Like your friend with the pony-tail. Valentina?'

She'd made me curious. 'How did you know that she had gone?'

'Because it was Broderick who fixed up the flight for her. The poor woman showed up at our place in a shocking state, all trembling and ashen-faced.'

That didn't sound like Valentina. 'Really?'

Julia nodded. 'Sweat dripping off her, and her hands were shaking so much she couldn't hold the cup of tea I tried to give her. It was horrible to watch. She'd clearly had a terrible experience, and it had freaked her out so much that she could barely speak. She only started to calm down when Broderick had made enough calls to get her on the next flight out.' Julia stared out over the bay. 'I was the one who drove her to the helipad. She was still in a state.'

'But what had *happened*?'

'She wouldn't say.' Julia made a face. 'Though I suspect I can guess, and I wouldn't be surprised if she wouldn't tell Broderick anything in case he thought she was crazy.'

I thought back to that dreadful feeling Julia and I

had shared while we were scrambling away from the pumping station into the safety of the car. 'Was it those things that weren't exactly there? If Valentina thought that she'd been seeing ghosts, she would have thought that she was going mad.'

Julia was still staring out across the wide band of water.

'She must have told you *something*,' I persisted.

'Nothing. We knew the firm was sending someone to make sure the last of the place was flattened. "Fit to abandon", they called it. We even saw the giant digger they'd sent down from Topane trundling past our place. It was the most *enormous* great thing!' She spread her hands wide. '*Massive.*'

'I'll bet.'

'Next thing we know, your Valentina is on our veranda, gabbling so fast that neither of us could follow – something about being bullied.'

'Valentina? *Bullied?* What, by the digger driver?'

Now Julia was giving me that old *Oh, Louie. Use your brain* look.

'You think that it was spirits.'

Julia smiled at me. 'Well, you and I both know those things are *pushy*.'

'So did you manage to explain?'

She shook her head. 'I tell you, she was in no state to listen.'

I thought back to that panic-making sense I'd had of being swarmed around and jostled – pretty well suffocated – by all those things that weren't exactly there. 'She's not the sort to understand it, anyway. It was the weirdest feeling I've ever had.'

We sat in silence, both of us remembering. Finally, Julia said, 'And since that day, of course, more of them will have gathered there.'

'And they'll be even more determined.'

'Yes. Even more determined. But to do what?'

'Oh, I know that,' I openly admitted. 'I know that.'

THIRTY-ONE

A larger hand around my own

'Your last job,' Toby had said. And if I'm honest, I had known at once that it concerned that shadow on the photo of the ridge. *Spi Ruaradh,* the ancient sacred place guarded on each side by those scary faces. I don't know why I was so sure of that. For all my hours and hours of listening, the Endlanders had told me only how their loved ones died. Not one of them had ever shared a word about anything else.

But there had been enough clues. Those two ghost sisters on the beach, asking about the causeway. All of those dripping people trudging in one direction along the road. Even the dog. And, at the pumping station itself, the gathering hordes that weren't exactly there but Julia and I had felt pressing impatiently round us. Their great-great-grandfathers might have been bullied into building hard up against the cavern in the ridge, blocking it totally; it was obvious that now these restless spirits of the dead wanted it opened again. Hadn't it been called The Causeway, after all? Causeway to where?

Creepy to think of, but not hard to guess.

And why should they ever put their faith again in the small cemetery they'd been given on the bay in order to replace their ancient way of dealing with the dead? One great wave comes along, and all their loved ones' bones and shrines are rudely sucked away. Why not go back to old and trusted tradition?

Now, while so many of the drowned still wandered about.

So, yes. I knew exactly what these wet souls wanted. And I knew it was up to me. I didn't dare risk going back down to the bay. Dad might catch sight of me, and send me to the bunkhouse to pack our stuff. He might not let me take time out to visit the pumping station one last time, and certainly not alone. And if he'd picked up more gossip – maybe heard that Valentina got in the helicopter in an awful state – he probably wouldn't want me going anywhere at all.

Toby had said I had a job to do over the ridge. If I told Dad anything about it, he would forbid me to go.

And there was no way I wanted to have to choose which of them to obey – my brother or my dad.

'Thanks, Tobes,' I muttered. 'Thanks a bunch.'

I'd clearly startled Julia. 'Sorry?'

I didn't try to explain. All I said was, 'Julia, if I come down on your side, will you give me a lift?'

She didn't bother to pretend she was surprised. 'Where? To the pumping station?'

'Please.'

She did give me a very beady look. 'Sure you know what you're doing?'

'Pretty sure.'

So, I went down with Julia on her side, back to her car. Without a word, she handed me a strange-looking key that Valentina had apparently pressed in her hand the night before, when the two of them parted at the helipad. Neither of us spoke on the drive. I think Julia knew that I was trying to summon up some confidence and courage. Still, it seemed no time at all before we drew up outside the ruins of the fence.

There was the digger, pointing directly at the ridge. And Julia was right. It was enormous. Massive.

We stared in silence till she asked, 'Do you even know how to get it started?'

'I probably can guess,' I told her bravely. 'But it won't matter anyhow. I'll get the help I need. One of them's sure to know.'

She didn't bother to ask what I meant. 'Well, should I come into the compound with you?'

'No, that's all right. But if you don't mind staying here…?'

She put her arm around me. 'Of course I'll stay. Good luck.'

'Thanks.'

I climbed out of the car and at once I could sense that there were crowds of them around me. I got the feeling they were vaguely hostile, too, until I climbed up in the giant digger, and settled in its torn old bucket seat.

I looked about, wondering where the key went.

My hand was pushed. There was no doubt about it. My hand was moved to the right place. But, unlike Valentina, I was glad of it. I honestly think, without the forceful help, I could have wasted hours, first looking for the lock, then, with the key refusing to turn either to left or right, unsure of what to do.

Instead, I felt a pulse under my forearm. Stronger and stronger it came, until I raised my elbow off the ledge and heard a tiny click. So, could the seat arm be raised?

It could. The moment I tugged, the arm flew up as if forced from beneath. My right hand was pushed back towards the key, which now agreed to turn. A buzzer sounded on the number pad above the lock. Clearly the digger had a built-in code.

I could have sat there for a week, except they knew. The tiny flashes – there, yet not exactly there – led me to each of the numbers in turn, then down to *Enter*. Then, with a sharp nudge from nowhere, I turned the key again, one more notch to the right.

No engine noise. But as I sat there, waiting, I was pressured into lowering the control arm back where it was when I climbed on the seat. I realised I was getting the hang of knowing what they wanted me to do, and this time when they made me try the key again, it turned yet another notch.

A tiny light flashed underneath the number pad. Obediently, I pressed that. The engine purred to life. And we were off.

I'll never know which of the restless spirits was so good at operating diggers. But I can claim no credit for the job we did. I only had to push or pull or turn whatever

I was made to push or pull or turn, all in a way and at a speed that was made easy for me. There might as well have been a larger hand around my own, keeping me right. Up swung the scoop and forward went the digger. The scoop tipped back. Its metal teeth gripped in the scree packed up against the cliff and effortlessly tugged the first heap of it free. Under the expert guidance I was getting, the digger trundled in reverse, the scoop swung to the side and dropped its load.

Over and over and over. I don't have any idea how long it took, or how many times that scoop scraped deep into the rocks and rubble that blocked their old, old causeway, *Spi Ruaradh*. Twice I saw Julia drawing close over the compound and raising her thumbs, all smiles, while shouting something that I couldn't hear over the roar of the digger.

I wasn't able to wave back. My arms still weren't my own.

At last, in front of me there was a sort of landslide. The scoop had pulled away so much of what was heaped against the entrance that all the rubble at the top began to slip. At the scoop's highest arc appeared a small, uneven opening, cloaked in a billowing grey dust that slowly cleared to show the top of the old passageway into the cave. I waited. There was a moment's pause, then suddenly the scoop changed tack, startling me with a new rhythm. It was no longer digging out the stones and rocks and earth, and swinging them around on to piles at the sides. Now it was simply hollowing out more to drag it forward, making a ramp.

Then, without warning, the digger rolled back one last time, further than before. The scoop swung up. My fingers were pushed forward one last time, to switch off the engine, and then became my own again.

Clearly it was all over. We were done.

The world fell silent all around, and suddenly my brother felt so real, so close to me, I could have reached for his hand. I know he was still at my side as I climbed down. I felt unsteady on my feet from the vibrations of the huge machine. Still, not even waiting for Julia to hurry over, I picked my way on all fours up the rubble of the ramp to peer in through the hole.

At first, I could barely make out what I saw through the unsettled clouds of dirt and dust. But there was nothing dank and stale about this cavern, blocked so thoroughly and for so long. Cold air was on my face. I could taste salt and smell the sea. I heard the burbling flow of that old underground stream not even the pumping station had been able to commandeer entirely. And, as I waited for the air to clear, I felt as if the barrier between some old world and the one I knew was swept away. A whistling filled my ears, and broken images streamed through my mind of tall, almost transparent figures rushing past as if, now, it was me, not them, who wasn't real enough to slow their surge towards the opened causeway. Frightened and buffeted, I tried to catch my breath. My knees and feet kept slipping on the open scree. It was as if a flurried wave was passing through me, over me and round me. Almost a stampede.

And then it was over at last. Like a wave that has flooded as far as it can up the beach, only to fall in lacy loops back over the shingle, the pandemonium in my head was dwindling. Across my mind now flickered strange, disjointed scenes as if I'd woken in a cinema to see the last few fleeting frames of some peculiar film I couldn't understand.

But I knew Toby was gone.

Part of me felt aggrieved he hadn't hung around, if only long enough to say, 'Bingo! You did it! Great job!' But now the silence round me felt so real it seemed to echo. Toby had gone for good, and I knew that I'd never hear his voice again unless I conjured it.

Why not? I'd done what he had wanted, after all. So, 'Happy now?' I asked.

I made him give the strangest answer. 'Only if you promise me that you will be, as well.'

Telling myself I would think more about that when I was on my own again, I slid unsteadily down the ramp and picked my way across the compound, over to where Julia was waiting.

THIRTY-TWO

Some dark cloud drifting away

Of course, I got a royal tongue-lashing for vanishing all afternoon. I didn't *dare* mention the digger. I rabbited on a bit about having climbed the ridge so I could take one last look at the bay, then bumping into Julia. And I suppose Dad just assumed the two of us had spent the whole time sitting in the sun and chatting.

We left the very next day, as soon as Dad had set in place what he called 'mopping-up' arrangements. We cadged a lift from someone driving to Topane. I stared out at the ever-shifting patchwork of green that seemed to be trying to swallow me into its darkness, but somehow, I felt washed with peace and light. As usual, sitting on my own behind two adults, I thought about my brother. But this time it was different. I wasn't *missing* him. I didn't feel, as I had always felt before, that something was *wrong* for him not to be at my side. He wasn't there, and I was thinking of him. But it was all right.

Along the roadside hung those dusty grey creepers I had thought so strange when, way back then, we had first driven to the bay. They just seemed normal now. So did the fact that there were no houses or roadside stores, almost no side turnings. I wondered what it must be like to grow up in such an isolated place, and that set me thinking about how I was going to feel when I was back at home, with Mum's friends always coming round, and Will dragging me out to make up the numbers on a scratch team here, or join him at the climbing wall. While I was at the bay, I'd had no sense of spending hours on my own. But, looking back, I realised that I had. A lot of that time while I was sitting there in the cabin, pretending to listen, I'd let my thoughts drift, summoned up memories and had my own quiet daydreams.

Things must have settled in me.

On the long bus ride back from Topane to Sachard, I tried to get things straight with Dad about what happened the last day. 'You know those hours I was gone?'

'Up on the ridge?'

'That's where I was for starters. Then Julia and I went down the other side. She drove me to the pumping station.'

'So *that's* why you were gone so long. Why didn't you say?'

I ignored that. 'The thing is, Dad, I got to drive the digger.'

His head spun round to search my face. He gave me *such* a warning look. 'Don't say a single word more,' he told me sharply. 'We keep employees' time schedules for years. If you so much as *hint* that you were allowed within fifty metres of that beast when it was working, that driver will lose his job.'

I wasn't sure I could explain, so I said nothing more. Dad sat there, fuming openly, probably not sure if he was mad at me for coming out with what he hoped was boastful rubbish, or at some unknown employee who'd let me climb in his cabin. I was quite glad when, ten minutes later, he'd calmed down enough to fall asleep.

He woke in a much better mood when we were nearly at Sachard. Realising that we would be meeting Mum in almost no time at all, I dared to ask, 'Do you feel better about Toby now?'

'Better?'

What was the best way to put it? I wasn't really asking him if things were fine. I wasn't even asking if he thought they ever would be. 'I suppose I'm asking if you maybe feel a bit less haunted by it all.'

He patted my knee, as if to let me know the question was all right with him.

'I talked to Hugo once or twice, you know. We talked about how disdainful some people are about Malouy, but he reckoned that, without even realising, pretty well everyone starts to deal with the loss of those they loved with some sort of supernatural thinking.'

'Supernatural thinking?'

'You know. You think you see them in the street. You think you hear their voice. You think they've come to you in dreams. And when I said, "So what's all that about?" Hugo replied that ghosts are important.'

I thought I knew what Hugo might have meant, but still I said, 'Important for what?'

'For forcing you to think things through. Hugo said ghosts are the embodiment of your regrets and guilt, and represent your deepest fears about how things had been between you and the one you loved.'

I couldn't help but feel a bit resentful. In all the time

that I'd been working for him, Hugo had never once said anything that thoughtful to me. Still, I was curious.

'What sort of deepest fears?'

'You know – that you let down the one who died. Didn't love them as much as you should have, or take enough care of them. Made wrong decisions. That sort of thing. They are, said Hugo, a sign of all your failings and your failures. That's why you see them. It's because part of you knows that, sooner or later, you're going to have to face all that.'

Curiously, I asked, 'Does that mean you now think that spirits might be *real*?'

He glanced my way. 'For heaven's sake, Louie! Of course they're not real. They're ghosts! And ghosts don't exist.'

So. My old Dad.

But he surprised me, then, by going back to my first question. 'Less haunted, though? I do feel as if the past is moving off at last, like some dark cloud drifting away. I feel as if a weight has lifted off my shoulders.' Again, he patted my knee. 'After your brother died, all I could think of wanting was for everything to be exactly how it was before. I knew it couldn't happen, but I still wanted it. Desperately badly.' He sighed.

'And now I recognise, even deep down inside me, that's never going to happen.' He stared out of the window at the outskirts of the little town. 'When Toby died, everything changed for ever. Everything will always be different. But I suppose I now believe that there will be good things to come.'

So my next question just spilled out. 'Like getting back with Mum?'

He grinned. 'Exactly. Yes. Like getting back with your mother.'

I had to ask. 'You still think that will happen?'

'Of course it'll happen.' He said the words just as he had that time before, with total confidence. 'I've always loved your mother. I always will. And she knows that. She'll have me back.'

THIRTY-THREE

The threads of our old life

She met us off the bus. 'My heavens!' she said to me. 'You look so *tanned*.' She turned to Dad. 'And you! You certainly lost some weight out there! You look so trim and fit!'

'All the better to hug you,' he said, and swung her round till she was begging him, 'Phil! I'm so dizzy. Stop it! Put me down!'

He held her till she'd steadied, then picked up both our bags. 'Where did you leave the car?'

She led us from the station.

Towards the end of the drive home, she made a point of telling Dad what she had made for supper, so it was obvious he was invited. It was a cheery enough meal. Dad didn't talk too much about broken turbines and jammed tappet cover gaskets, and I said nothing about restless spirits. But still we talked all through. Mum told us some of the things that she'd been doing while we were away. And by the time Dad and I carried the last of the dishes to the sink, it must have been pretty late.

He picked up his jacket and bag and turned to me. 'I'll leave you here, shall I?'

Mum beat me to an answer. 'You're certainly not taking Louie off tonight! He's only just got back! I'd practically forgotten what he looks like.'

In spite of that, she sent me off to bed the moment he was gone. 'You look *exhausted.*' I don't know where the next day went. I must have slept through most of it. So it was not till the day after, when I went back to Dad's, that I saw what had happened in Toby's room.

I'd dumped my bag on my own bed, thinking how, in the old days when I came back from any trip, my brother would be hanging over the bannisters, raring to start the inquisition. 'Hi, Louie! What was it like? Was the food any good? Is it true Jeffer's brother got sent home before the end? How were the teachers?' So it was with a fierce stab of missing him that I went across the landing and pushed open his door.

All change.

Everything of Toby's was gone. Where his bed used to be, a set of shelves had been set up. The chipped old table where he had glued his models had vanished, and in its place stood a sleek black computer desk with a new pinboard above. All of his posters had been taken down. The dingy yellow walls were now sky blue, the tatty curtains nowhere to be seen. Above the open window now, there was a roller blind.

And on one wall were photos, loads of them, all newly framed, and all with Toby in them. Just Toby. Toby with me. Toby with all of us. Toby on Dad's shoulders. Toby, Toby, Toby. Toby at every age he'd ever been: a sleeping baby, on his toddler trike, in the nursery school paddling pool, standing with Jimmy St George in their brand new cub-scout uniforms, dressed as a pirate in last year's school play.

Even astride the bright blue racing bike on which he died.

I'd stopped short in the doorway. Behind me, Dad was racing up the stairs. 'You've gone in. You've seen what your mother's done.'

I couldn't speak, just nodded.

He slid a comforting arm round my shoulders. 'Pretty big change, eh? Startling.'

I found my voice at last. 'Did you know she was doing it?'

He shook his head. 'No. Not at all. Bit of a shock.' After a moment, he added, 'Well, obviously, she has a key, and I expected her to keep an eye on things while we were gone. It's her house too. But certainly I didn't think that she'd do something like this.'

I wasn't sure if I should ask him, but I did. 'So do you *mind*?'

'Do I *mind*?' The words came out as if the idea hadn't yet occurred to him. He stood in silence, staring at the wall of photographs, then turned to look at all the other new stuff. 'If I am honest,' he said, 'my first thought wasn't about the room at all. I mean, I do think it was very brave of her. I know I couldn't have done it – not to save my life. Gone through the photos like that? I would have been a wreck. I would have been a puddle of tears just at the thought of it. I simply don't know how she did it.'

It wasn't cold, but still he walked across to pull the window closed. Maybe it was because he didn't want me looking at him when he said what came out next. 'But my first thought was, if your mum's done this, that must mean that she's coming back.' He flipped the

266

window latch and turned to face me. 'So, I was *happy*.'

What was I to say?

Now he was making for the door. 'I'll leave you to it,' he said. 'It takes some getting over, seeing all these photographs.'

It certainly did. I must have cried for half an hour or more, all the time thinking that probably my dad had done that too, that first night when he'd come home by himself. I wondered why she hadn't thought to warn us. Mean of her. Horrible! But then I thought maybe she'd done it weeks ago, when I first left for the bay. Maybe it slipped her mind that neither of us knew about this sort of shrine that she'd made for my brother.

Finally, I pulled myself together. Shrine it might be. And a huge shock. But soon, I knew, having it this way would be a thousand times better than coming in and seeing it the way it was before – almost how Toby left it on that last morning of his life – the same green duvet on the bed, his clothes still in the cupboards, the books that he'd been reading stacked on the table.

I checked my face for tear tracks, and went downstairs. Dad must have been waiting for me. He was at the kitchen table, facing the door and doing nothing. 'Okay?'

'Okay.'

He waited just a moment, in case I wanted to say more, then broke the silence. 'Up for a supermarket shop?'

'I think so, yes.' (Better than staying in the house and being tempted to look at the photos again.)

So off we went. As soon as we'd backed out of the narrow gate, and he could pay attention, I asked him, 'Dad, do you really think that wall of photos means that Mum is coming home?'

'Yes,' he said. 'I am quite sure of it. And I don't think it will be long.'

And he was right, as usual. Maybe Dad's engineering skills helped him know, not just how some things work, but how they're going to work out. Mum came home a few days later. First, she showed up just before supper one evening, carrying an overnight bag. Next morning, while I was at school, the two of them went back to fetch the stuff that she and I kept at the flat she'd rented. The day after that they both went over one last time to clean it so they could hand back the keys.

I stayed at home, working my way through all the Saturday jobs that Mum had put on the list. (I get through them much faster now I don't waste time arguing with Toby about which of us should do what.) Later, while Dad was trying to fit the stuff from Mum's freezer in ours, I picked up a giant pizza and said hopefully, 'Why don't you leave this out? We could have this tonight.'

'Sure that you two of you can manage it?'

That startled me. 'Why, where will you be?'

'Picking up Miles's next job because he's fallen out with Valentina and left.'

'What was the quarrel about?'

He sighed. 'She's had a bee in her bonnet about him from the day she got back. The lad can't do anything right.' I think, if I'd not been with him and Valentina in the Endlands, Dad might have left it there. He's always felt uncomfortable gossiping about colleagues, even to Mum. But I suppose he reckoned, since I'd been a part of things, he should explain. 'The thing is, Miles still claims that eerie things were going on. He still goes on that website – what's it called?'

'*UncannyBay.*'

'And tells us everything. And that is driving Valentina crackers. She thinks it's time he gave up on this silly ghost business.'

I trod as carefully as I could. 'So what does Valentina think was happening out there?'

He looked surprised I'd even asked the question. 'Well, obviously, nothing. A few people, very deeply disturbed by all the shocking things that they'd experienced, imagining things that weren't there.'

It was his sheer dismissiveness that made me say, 'She left in enough of a hurry herself.'

'True. But she at least admits she'd got into a state. Some sort of stress thing, after going back to where we were in the earthquake. She says that nothing that she thought she felt could have been *real*. She realised that as soon as she got back.' Dad slid the the last of Mum's frozen meals into the space he'd somehow managed to create, and closed the freezer door. 'Frankly, the way the two of them were sniping at one another all this week, it's probably just as well that Miles has gone.'

It was a quiet few days. I think that Mum had finally realised that I was fine being alone in the house when I got home before she was back from work. I helped her clear out the shed. We went to see one of the films Will had refused to see again. We worked our way through the nicest meals in the freezer. 'Sensible, really. Now things are much less crammed.'

I felt that every day I made more progress. One of my favourite teachers, Ms Cresswell, came back from working in another school. She'd been gone nearly two years and ran into me in the corridor. 'Hey, Louie. Good to see you! How come your brother didn't show up for the swimming trials last night?'

Ms Arnott happened to be right behind her. Taking Ms Cresswell's arm, she steered her firmly into the nearest classroom, and I walked on. I really, really loved my brother Toby. And I still do. But I no longer have to dive in the lavatories and hide in a cubicle. I wasn't late for my next class. I even managed to get on with my work.

But it did prompt me to go on *UncannyBay* that evening. Mum caught me scrolling through. As ever when she found me looking at a screen, she was suspicious. 'What's that you're wasting your time on?'

'Nothing much.'

And I decided that was true. Oh, there were a few more uploads of peculiar moving shadows and strange, flickering lights. A taxi driver from Topane talked of a woman who'd asked to be driven to the bay but shifted along the seat till he could no longer see her in the mirror. And when he got there she was gone, and the back seat was soaked in sea water.

Another creepy story. But very little that was new, and nothing as unnerving as what I'd seen. Next morning I asked Will if he kept up with going on the site, and wasn't much surprised when he said he no longer bothered.

Early on the last morning before Dad came back, Mum caught me standing in the room that she now called 'the office'. I'd had a dream of Toby the night before. We had been quarrelling about a shiny bell that I'd accused him of unscrewing from my bike and fixing on his own. The dream had been so vivid that I'd been wondering if it could be a memory, and had come in to see if any of the bikes in the photos on the wall had had that sort of bell.

Mum hesitated in the doorway, then came to join me, waving a hand at the wall. 'Louie, I have been thinking that I owe you an apology. I should have thought to warn you about this when you came back. Your dad says that it was a shock.'

'It was.'

She made a rueful face. 'I really didn't think. You

see, I'd spent so much time in here sorting things out that I'd forgotten it would catch the two of you totally off guard. I am so sorry.'

'It's okay.' Somehow that didn't seem enough to say, and so I forced myself to add, 'I think it's probably a really good idea.'

'Do you?'

Why not be honest? 'Well,' I said. 'Not quite yet. But I know I will.'

And in a way, just having said that did make looking at the photos easier, as if I didn't need to feel good about them yet. I could just look at them and know that Toby was dead and gone, and these were days we'd had together. What was so wrong with setting up a sort of shrine to remember the good times? I think about my brother every day, and I'm still proud of him. (Even when dead and restless, Toby never did turn into one of those stubbornly unappeasable Spirits of Spite so many in the cabins feared.) I can still conjure him up whenever I want to talk to him or ask his advice. And there have been no more of those unnerving, uninvited orders out of the blue. Sometimes I wonder if, like Valentina, I may come to think that I'd imagined those. And the dead, dripping figures. But I will never forget the sense

I had of all those spirits pressing in, that feeling that the everyday world had somehow cracked open, and my conviction that those strange and unseen figures had finally been able to escape down their old causeway.

I learned a lot out on the bay. All the time I'd been in that cabin, listening, I'd heard those men and women talk about the tidal wave as if the massive damage and destruction, and all those deaths, were unbelievable. Almost absurd. It *couldn't* have happened that way, they seemed to tell me endlessly. It was *impossible*. What happened simply couldn't be true.

So disbelief, I've realised, can run two ways.

Some day, I'll want to talk to Dad about what happened at the bay. But not right now. Not just because he'll think it was just some crazy vision in my brain, and go to great lengths to explain the workings of the mind and how I must have ended up as good as haunting myself. More because I'm worried I might raise different ghosts. That cloud of numbness and horror that had been paralysing Dad is finally gone, and he has fought his way out of the fog of silence he'd lived in since my brother's death. Now he can face the photographs of Toby, and doesn't flinch when Mum says Toby's name. That's why she's back. And now we're picking up the threads of our old life, I am determined not to make things difficult.

We will talk some day. We must, or it will harden into something we can never talk about. I've seen the damage that can do. Our little family has had enough of that. So, yes, I'll definitely want to get things straight with Dad one day.

But not right now. I've had enough of ghosts.

Behind the book

Any author will tell you they've been asked to write in particular ways ('Oh, please write a *scary* story!') or about particular things ('Could you do a book set in outer space?'). But I'm not the only writer who has to wait for both the topic, and the idea of how to go about it, to fall in line with one another – a bit like needing not just your body but also the right clothes before you're ready to go out.

I'd always wanted to write about the awful, awful fall-out for any family when there has been a death that really shouldn't have taken place. It happens a lot more often than you might think, and is more difficult for everyone to deal with than almost anything else that can be imagined. One person's way of dealing with it may seem strange, or unfeeling, to another. Too often, families end up falling apart.

Then, out of the blue, I read an article about the very, very strange events reported by the survivors of a massive disaster. As so often at the start of a novel, things shifted in my brain. I suddenly thought of a way in which I could explore, not just the the ways in which grief can affect this person, or that family, but also how entire communities can be turned upside down.

I know the author's job is basically just to provide 'a good read'. But, over and above that, those of us who write for young people very often find that we're hoping to interpret this complicated, often intimidating, world to those who read us. Most of us took huge comfort, and learned a lot about ourselves and others, from reading books. Sometimes it's realising you're not the only one in the world ever to have had this problem. 'That's how it is for me. That's how I feel!' Sometimes it broadens your understanding. 'Yes, I bet that's exactly how it would have been.'

We hope we're offering something in the nature of a hope to cling to, a line to take, even a way to go. The writer Susan Sontag once said, 'I think the most useful thing that I can do with my fiction is to increase the sense of the *complexity* of things.' That's what I hope I'm doing in this book.

Anne Fine, July 2021

Anne Fine is one of Britain's most distinguished writers for children. She has twice won both the Carnegie Medal and the Whitbread Children's Book of the Year Award, as well as the Guardian Children's Fiction Prize, the Smarties Prize and numerous other regional and foreign awards. She has twice been voted Children's Author of the Year. The BBC have screened adaptations of several of her books, and her novel *Madame Doubtfire* became a Hollywood film.

Anne was Children's Laureate from 2001-2003, during which time she set up **bookplates.uk**, a website that offers a host of freshly designed and freely downloadable bookplates to enthuse young readers to form their own home libraries from the second-hand books around them.

Anne's work has been translated into forty-five languages. In 2003 she was made a Fellow of the Royal Society of Literature and awarded an OBE. Anne has two daughters and four grandchildren, and lives in County Durham.

You can read more about her work at **annefine.co.uk**